CHEKHOV'S
JOURNEY

CHEKHOV'S JOURNEY

IAN WATSON

Carroll & Graf Publishers, Inc.
New York

Copyright © 1983 by Ian Watson

First Carroll & Graf edition 1989

Carroll & Graf Publishers, Inc.
260 Fifth Avenue
New York, NY 10001

Library of Congress Cataloging-in-Publication Data

Watson, Ian, 1943–
    Chekhov's journey / Ian Watson. — 1st Carroll & Graf ed.
      p.   cm.
    ISBN 0-88184-523-X : $16.95
    1. Chekhov, Anton Pavlovich, 1860–1904, in fiction, drama,
poetry, etc. I. Title.
PR6073.A863C47   1989
823'.914—dc20   89-37988
                                      CIP

Manufactured in the United States of America

For Brian Stableford

One

ANTON HUDDLED IN his sheepskin jacket and military-style leather raincoat. As the buggy jolted him along through the Siberian night, numbly he watched last year's grass burning off the frosted fields.

Tongues of flame laced the earth with flickering red and gold, which faintly illuminated occasional groves of birch trees. Yet the night immediately stole any warmth away. The Road was frozen, hard as iron. Driving along was more like lurching over an endless series of suits of armour laid side by side.

How long had they been travelling? Was it five hours, or eight? The horses were tramping like brainless machines, and driver Volodya had long since gone into a trance. But Anton hadn't yet learned the trick of sleeping through this sort of punishment.

Maybe Volodya had died, a few hours ago? Imagine being driven for tens of versts by a dead body without even realizing it!

Soon the sun would rise. By the afternoon the Road would become a churned-up quagmire. Where it broadened, on its way through villages, it would be a river of mud with houses on both banks . . .

Abruptly thunder drummed from the darkness ahead. Hooves, wheels!

Within seconds a troika of the Imperial Postal Service came dashing out of the night—three horses abreast, and no intention of yielding to anything on the road.

Even as Anton cried a warning, Volodya was jerking on the reins. The old codger wasn't dead, after all. He hauled the team and buggy over to the right, just as the troika thundered past, missing them by a hand's span.

As Volodya and Anton swung round to curse the troika on its way, they spied—bearing down from the darkness behind—a second juggernaut, returning full tilt towards Tomsk. This second troika careered past the first, heading directly towards them. And worse! Behind it, a third troika charged in pursuit.

Volodya lashed his team with the reins. "God save us!" he howled.

With their usual nervy stupidity, the horses swung the buggy the wrong way; and it blocked the Road entirely.

What had been till a moment earlier an empty void was suddenly filled with a chaos of crashing wood and whinnying, rearing horseflesh. Briefly their own buggy stood up on end. A moment later Anton found that he wasn't sitting in it at all, but was lying sprawled on the ground, bombarded by his luggage.

Scrambling up, he raced aside. "Stop, damn you, stop!" he screamed down the road.

But the third troika hurtled towards them, pell-mell. Its driver was a dark lump, probably fast asleep. A few seconds later it too crashed into the tangle. Again, horses reared, shafts cracked and harness snapped. Yokes tumbled to the ground over trampled baggage.

Then, for a few moments, everything was so still that Anton believed he had gone deaf. In the east, ever so faintly, dawn was beginning to glow.

At least two of the drivers must have been tumbled out of their dreams into this nightmare of bruises and cold. Though the occurrence could hardly be unique, it took them a short while to work out what had happened. But then they and Volodya squared up to each other in the gloom—and the driver of the first troika ran ʾup to add his own contribution.

"You were asleep, you buggering fool!"

"You lying clip-prick, *I* was awake. The other two fuckers weren't!"

"You couldn't drive a team of rabbits, Grandpa!"

Crazed by the invective being bellowed on all sides, the horses milled and collided hysterically. Idiot creatures that they were, they reared and kicked and tried to bite holes in each other's necks. Their hooves pummelled broken shafts and jumbled luggage. And nobody made the slightest effort to calm the beasts, or drag the damaged vehicles apart, or clear their spilled contents aside. Obsessed with abuse, the four drivers merely swore at each other endlessly, blaming and blaspheming and accusing each other of being Jews and sodomists and lunatics.

Anton stood by in fear and fury; he wondered if he ought to pull out his revolver and discharge it over their heads to restore order. And cold flames crackled in the fields, as anaemic daylight spilled slowly from the horizon . . .

Only when the drivers were quite hoarse did they deign to back off and begin tidying up. Volodya had to commandeer the straps from Anton's trunk to tie up their own shafts and harness. Eventually, after what seemed like two hours, their buggy crept on its way . . .

The next post station was versts away, and half-a-dozen times they had to stop to refasten the shafts or harness which easily broke loose again. The Road was already becoming slightly soggy in the mocking sunshine, though ice still crusted the puddles.

Flights of ducks beat their way overhead, provoking Anton's belly to a rage of hunger. To stop his own tripes consuming themselves, he bit off a chunk of the sausage he'd been fool enough to buy a hundred versts back; and instantly regretted it. The meat smelled of peasant feet unwrapped after six months, and tasted like a dog's tail dipped in tar and shit. Hastily he spat out the vile mouthful and flushed his tastebuds with vodka, which was pretty foul too—sharp and oily. Thousands of crumbs had worked their way down into his underpants, but he couldn't find a single whole crust of bread in any of his pockets.

True, a bottle of finest cognac reposed in his baggage. Kuvshinnikov, the complaisant cuckold, had presented this to him

9

with a fine flourish, to be quaffed on the shores of the Pacific. He wouldn't be surprised if the bottle had been smashed during the collision. Well, at least his gun hadn't gone off and shot him in the stomach . . .

Longing for the barren oasis of the next village, Anton stared ahead.

Curiously, he didn't feel at all unwell. He was starving, and exhausted to the point of hallucination. But his head no longer ached with migraines, and his piles had cleared up since Ekaterinburg. Even his cough was better. As for gastritis, bye-bye to that.

A good Christian might have said that all his routine ailments were really devils—but lately the going had got too rough for them; so they had all decamped . . .

Salvation was in sight at last!

Wooden cabins, straggling along both sides of the Road far ahead. An onion dome sitting on a little wooden church . . .

Buoyed up, Anton became aware of the jingle of their own harness bells. Was it a merry note? No, it was just a noise . . . He began to daydream lustfully of sturgeon bouillabaisse. Ah yes, flavoured with sorrel and mushrooms . . .

Fat chance of that!

Two

"IN THE YEAR 1890, as yet, there was no Trans-Siberian Railway to ride on. Chained convicts still trudged for months through seas of mud and bitter frosts—into eternal exile!"

Sergey Gorodsky looked up from his notebook to see how his words were coming over.

"We'll use a montage of still photos," he added. Sergey was a stocky man, with a crusty loaf of a head. A peak of close-cropped stubbly golden hair, rising above a pocked and sallow face, made it seem as if his crust had split in the baking.

The sudden dark silhouette of some hungry bird beat against the great, drape-clad windows of the Artists' Retreat, then darted away; and Sergey stared out down the hill, as though a line of raggy prisoners might suddenly materialise from amidst the snowy larch trees. However, the steep valley remained unpeopled. The blue wooden faces of the various dachas were all shuttered tight, and no vehicle moved along the road, though it had been snow-ploughed.

What the hell had become of Dr Kirilenko? He ought to have been here ages ago.

"Hang on," said Felix Levin. "It won't do."

Presiding genius of the Stanislavsky Film Unit of Krasnoyarsk, Felix was as personable as Sergey was ill-favoured. He could have been an ageing gigolo, only slightly run to seed. His dark wavy hair, worn rather long, was streaked with silver. He kept a French battery-razor in the pocket of his Italian suit at all times, and used it thrice a day. Once something of a coxcomb with the girls, for the past ten years he had been busy sublimating personal style into committed art. Sergey, in his dingier and more envious moments, pegged him as someone who had gone to bed with so many young women that they had all melted together eventually into one collective, sexless Muse which whispered, now, political endearments. Put one way, he had matured. Put another, he had run out of his former supply of juice—and a good thing too.

Felix slapped the side of the saggy armchair in which he was sprawling elegantly; the blow raised a puff of dust and fibre. Most of the furniture was equally ancient.

"Sorry, won't do at all! That suggests the railway was built to get rid of people. Not to open up Siberia as a positive step. You must watch your nuances." Not so many years ago, as they all knew, there had been many large labour camps in the vicinity of Krasnoyarsk . . .

"Well, we can hardly say that the Czar's government went in for nation building!"

"Oh, agreed. But you're still equating Siberia with exile. Look, an underlying theme of the film has to be how Siberia spelled *space for development*. Though this didn't occur in a properly planned way till later on . . . And as a sub-theme, there could well be a hint that the Siberia of tomorrow's world will literally be space. Outer space—the asteroid belt, the moons of Jupiter! Where a socialist attitude's the only possible one; everyone pitching in, or else it's lethal. We mustn't associate space with punishment."

In exasperation Sergey threw down his notebook on the disintegrating leather sofa, which he shared with Mikhail Petrov the actor.

"I fail to see how we can dispense with the convicts! Damn it all, they're the reason why Chekhov crossed Siberia—"

"It's just the balance of words and images."

"—to visit the convict colony on Sakhalin!"

"You're the writer, Sergey. Surely you can see that?"

"But our film isn't about colonising the bloody asteroids! It's about the writer Chekhov—to commemorate the anniversary of his journey, right? It's about a watershed in one artist's life—"

"A watershed brought about by an act of social commitment. Plus: the experience of launching himself out across untold space, far from the hothouse of Moscow literary life. Metaphor, see? But we mustn't be 'arty', however beautiful our intentions are. This is a scientific film—first, because of the sort of person Chekhov was, and secondly because we'll be using Dr Kirilenko's hypnosis technique. Science is a sub-text of the film."

Actor Mikhail tossed back his head, as though to indicate that all this had nothing to do with him. A faint smile puckered the corner of his mouth; idly he inspected the shabby elegance of the room.

It had once been a reception room, for prior to becoming a rural appendix of the People's Palace of Culture in Krasnoyarsk, decades earlier, this Retreat had been the Summer home of some aristocratic exile who had been allowed to take his wealth to Siberia. The room had little connexion with a present time which included the likelihood of colonising space. A threadbare oriental carpet covered most of the floor. An antique mahogany table was draped in oilskin. Aspidistras sprouted from glazed terracotta pots. And the light bulbs hummed constantly, as if electricity were just newly discovered and the secret consisted in imprisoning hot little devils in glass bottles. Lampshades, of tasselled sallow-silk, were stained by age and the heat of the bulbs. The room could easily have been a stage set for some last-century drama. How very appropriate.

Mikhail straightened the right side of his moustache with his index finger. It was a *good* mannerism.

"Really, fellows, all this business about a watershed! I mean, those hills out there are watersheds—for a fact. But old Antosha was such a secretive chap. I ain't got the foggiest why he set off across Siberia."

"Come off it," said Sergey. "We know a whole host of reasons."

"Well, that's just it, ain't it? Which was the one that tipped the balance?"

"There doesn't have to be a single reason, shining like a beacon. There wouldn't be in one of his plays."

"Sure. The main business of all the plays is sheer dither. Oh, what's to be done? Oh, if only we could . . . But we can't. There'll be paradise on Earth in another hundred years. Perhaps. But as for now, oh dear me, what's the point?"

"It *is* a hundred years later," Felix reminded Mikhail sharply. Mikhail tipped his head still further back; softly he laughed.

Despite himself Felix nodded in approval. The Film Unit had discovered Mikhail through a nation-wide Chekhov Look-Alike Contest. Mikhail had been in repertory in Gorki, and he was endearingly second-rate. Which was ideal . . .

"Drivel!" cried Sergey. "Nina runs off to go on the stage, in *The Seagull*, doesn't she? Duels get fought. Revolvers pop off. People do predict an earthly paradise of work and honesty and good will—and they mean it. People make wild declarations of passion."

"Which all come to nothing. And oh, those blessed revolvers! After our Anton got back from Sakhalin, he always loaded them with blanks."

"Blanks? What do you mean?"

"Just look how he revised *The Wood Demon*. Second time round, Vanya just misses—at point-blank range. So what exactly did wind our darling Antosha up to that final notch so that he flew thousands of kilometres—oops, pardon me, thousands of versts—clear across Siberia? Maybe he did it to purge himself of hysteria? The same hysteria that screws up his Ivanov, and makes the play *Ivanov* a pretty rotten one."

"Ivanov's energies weren't being put to constructive use," said Felix mildly.

"As yours are?" enquired Sergey.

Felix was about to squash this sally; but his aggrieved look changed to one of disbelief—for Mikhail had pulled a pistol out of his jacket pocket. He pointed it at the window.

"Bang," he said.

"For God's sake, man—-!"

"How the Devil—!"

Mikhail twirled the pistol round his finger, cowboy style.

"It's just a prop. Found it in the lumber-room, I did, stuffed down one of those baskets. So I thought to myself, if old Antosha had one in his pocket, so should I."

"Put it away, you fool!" bawled Sergey.

"Yes, do put it away, there's a good fellow—before *she* gets back." Now that the initial shock was over, Felix seemed quite amused.

Mikhail returned the gun to his pocket. "We don't know anything for sure."

"Ah, but we will once we make the film," said Felix.

At this moment Sonya Suslova came back into the room. Opening her blue eyes wide in apologetic perplexity, she shook her head.

"I phoned the Psychiatric Institute, but Dr Kirilenko hasn't been *there* . . ."

Mikhail regarded those expressive eyes of hers with amusement. It was a curious phenomenon, often noted by him, that your average Svetlana or Natasha tended to exaggerate her mannerisms in the presence of theatrical folk—as though she imagined that actors were in the business of pulling funny faces and were always on the look-out for some suitable facial tic to be immortalised. 'Look, 'Tasha, that's how I scratch my nose! He's got me off to a tee.' Whereas men just as often repressed their affectations out of *amour propre*, not wishing to be parodied.

Mikhail had seen this syndrome oodles of times; here it was again. And Dr Suslova a psychiatrist, too!

"Maybe his taxi broke down—or skidded!" Sonya registered alarm.

She was a chunky blonde with sensual lips and nostrils which would have been sensual, too, had nasal copulation been in vogue; perhaps she picked her nose in private. By contrast, her knitted two-piece was severe: a double corset of woollen chain-mail.

15

She had left the double doors open. "Osip!" Felix called out. "Can we all have some more tea?"

An answering loud grunt from somewhere along the passage indicated that the caretaker had heard.

Sergey recovered his notebook and riffled through it. "How about this, then? On April 21st 1890 Anton Chekhov left Moscow on a journey little short of heroic, dah-di-dah . . . period photo of the station. Some family and friends accompanied him as far as Yaroslavl. Photo of Levitan in his cocky hat and dandy togs. How about a photo of Levitan's mistress?"

"You'd have to show Sophia Kuvshinnikova's husband too," said Felix. "Could get complicated, eh?"

"Okay, forget her. Of these friends, only the eccentric lady astronomer Olga Kundasova carried on as far as Perm. Photo of a steamer on the Volga. Or the Kama."

"Carried on?" Mikhail winked at Sonya. "Didn't she just?—much to Anton's bewilderment. Oh, didn't he understand the ladies beautifully in his art? But in life, ah . . . perhaps he understood them all too well?"

Dr Suslova made a great fuss of seating herself, on an overstuffed divan. She plumped up and down, raising dust.

"Actually," Mikhail went on slyly, "in his opinion Kundasova ate like a horse. Chomp, chomp, chomp: a machine for champing oats . . ."

Three

THE FIRST BOON of the post station was an authentic toilet, located off the hallway. Amazingly there was even a supply of toilet paper; torn sheets of the *Siberian Herald* were spitted on a rusty hook. Anton used two of these for their destined purpose and folded another one into his pocket for later reference.

And that was all he took— because stuff just didn't seem to get nicked along the Road. Not if you were a *bona fide* traveller. Footpads and tramps and escaping convicts murdered and robbed each other blind without a second thought. They would kill an old peasant woman just to tear her skirt up for puttees to keep their legs warm. But genuine voyagers seemed to be protected by some ingrained instinct, though this could hardly be ascribed to a sense of decency. Conceivably it all harked back to the time of the Mongols. Maybe the yellow Asiatic overlords had decreed vicious tortures for anybody who interfered with a tax route, and a folk memory lingered on. Maybe he could write about this in his next article for Suvorin?

After relieving his bowels and bladder, Anton hied himself round to the stables, where three horses snuffled in their stalls. But there was no sign of any decent carriage or buggy to hire for the next stage, only one wreck of a cart.

A body lay snoring in the straw. The ostler's head was a beetroot, cropped to the scalp because of erysipelas. In vain Anton nudged the man with his boot. Having failed to kick life into the fellow, he returned to the post station to kick up a fuss instead.

Which he did as to the manner born, blustering and cursing for a full fifteen minutes. In the end he conceded that he might *just* be prepared to pay a little extra to winkle out some proper transport from wherever it was hidden. Emerging, he discovered that all his baggage had already been dumped in the street outside the door.

Volodya he found in the inn next to the post station. The old codger was trying to wheedle a drink out of the bloated innkeeper. The innkeeper, disdaining him, was shouting at his serving slut to dig herself out from behind the kitchen stove.

Cockroaches scuttled everywhere on the dining room walls. Though in other respects this place was a paragon of cleanliness, compared with Great Russian inns. It didn't stink of sweat, fart, vomit and rancid sunflower oil. Conceivably, too, the army of cockroaches was a hygienic improvement—they fed on bugs.

What's more, the innkeeper didn't belch into Anton's face; he merely yawned.

"There ain't a scrap to eat," the man protested. "We're cleaned out. I dunno why you're bothering me!"

However, Anton had learned the style. After a few days' travel in these parts, all your brain seemed capable of was rancour and malice. Promptly he lounged in a chair, hoisted his feet up on the table and began to roll a cigarette.

"I'm not shifting from here till you serve me something—so you might as well get your skates on!"

"That last lot cleaned us out, the greedy pigs. Well, they *did*, an' all."

Anton stared meaningfully at the innkeeper's swollen belly. Obviously the man was a hog, who kept all the best food for himself.

"I could manage some tea," conceded the hog.

"I'm not drinking brick dust, d'you hear? You can stuff it. How about some hot soup? With some fresh bread? What have you got, eh? Just leave out the corned beef!"

"Well, I could manage some milk soup—maybe with an egg whipped in it."

"You can stuff that, too! Haven't you got any fresh meat, man?

18

Fish, fowl, I don't care. It took me all eternity to get here, and don't think for a moment that I'm going to ask you for a bed with its zoo-full of wild life. I'm riding on. But not until I've swallowed something better than milk soup!"

A cunning sneer appeared on the innkeeper's face.

"Would your honour care for *duck* soup?"

Anton allowed himself, once again, to be gulled.

He sustained himself on nips of vodka till the soup arrived, approximately an hour later. The serving girl actually spread a tablecloth and brought the soup bowl without sticking her thumb in it. She also brought bread: a crisp, golden, fluffy dream!

Alas, the soup was a gruel of mud with raw onions floating in it. He spooned around: only the chopped-up gizzard and unwashed rectum of the duck seemed to be included in the recipe.

True to form, as soon as he had taken his first foul sip, a driver arrived from the village with news that his honour's carriage was awaiting him, this very moment. Snatching up some bread to sustain him through the coming fray, Anton hurried outside—and was confronted by a farm cart with a bed of dirty straw, harnessed to two nags.

He raged. "I'm not riding in that bloody thing! I need a proper carriage with a seat! A buggy will do fine."

"It's all there is, Sir."

"Liar! You're wasting your own time, never mind mine. Go and get a decent vehicle this moment. I know there's one—that layabout in the stable told me."

This couldn't go on! It was plain as the nose on his face that he would be forced to buy his own rattletrap in Tomsk, at ruinous cost to his finances . . .

In the end he agreed to a price which was sheer robbery; and off went the villager, whistling as he led the nags away, no doubt to the knacker, while Anton tramped indoors again to his soup. And of course all the duck grease had congealed by now. A layer of fatty ice lay upon an undrinkable cold pond.

19

Staring into this wretched mirror, his thoughts drifting, Anton found himself remembering . . .

The Novel . . . Ah yes, that novel he was supposed to be writing! The Big One. *Tales From the Lives of My Friends* . . . A young chap condemned to Siberia for armed rebellion; a police chief who despised his uniform; numerous atheists . . . a cast of dozens. Would he ever finish it, even as a set of separate stories? The embryo book seemed as far distant as the Moon right now. From this wretched inn he saw it through the wrong end of a mental telescope; the last few weeks had shrunk this magnum opus into insignificance.

Thrusting the soup aside, he stuffed his mouth with bread and filled his pockets, removing his notebook from one of them. While he waited for the villager to come back he scribbled the truth about Siberian post stations—so that he could mail the piece to *New Times* from Tomsk and pay off a bit more of his advance from Alexey Sergeyevich Suvorin . . .

20

Four

PRESENTLY OSIP, THE caretaker and general factotum, brought in the tea. His arrival prompted Sonya to leap up and rush to the window, as if this action would automatically bring a taxi into view.

"I really don't know what's keeping the Doctor," she said, quite superfluously, when nothing occurred.

Mikhail cleared his throat. "Dear lady, punctuality is a form of hysteria . . .

"I mean," he went on blithely, "it's hysterical to be exactly on time, ain't it? Take me for instance: last week I promised to meet this guy Ilya at the People's Palace. So I turned up on time, just a couple of minutes late. Of course Ilya didn't turn up so sharpish. I puffed one cigarette then another, and by the time he *did* show up—and he was only twenty minutes late—I was in such a stew that I just walked straight past the poor sod without a word. You ought to have seen his face! You remind me of him."

Sonya realized that she was staring in dumb wonder at this handsome young man with the high forehead and the whispy beard. She flushed with chagrin.

"What is time, anyway?" rhapsodized Mikhail, his hands spread wide. "What is time to a lump of rock hurtling between the stars?" He smirked. "Don't panic, I'm just doing my Antosha trick. Wait till I get my pince-nez on! Did you know that he was short-sighted in one eye, and far-sighted in the other one? Goodness, that must account for a lot! Oh, and don't let's forget this little scar up here." He tapped his forehead. "Collected this souvenir when I was a kid, I did. Bashed my noddle on a rock, diving into the Black Sea."

21

Sonya gazed at Mikhail's flawless brow, trying to perceive what wasn't there.

"I do wish you'd stop going on about 'Antosha'," complained Sergey. "The Siberian trip marks the transition from the frivolous young hack, Antosha, to the mature artist Anton. The trip was a rite of passage."

"So that's what it was?" And Mikhail stage-whispered lugubriously across the room to Sonya: "But I *am* frivolous—that's the trouble, from a dramatic point of view. I ain't no Meyerhold, see? Just the spit'n'image of old Anton Pavlovich."

"But you'll do, so long as your talent can be augmented?" Sonya nodded. "I shouldn't worry about it. Dr Kirilenko has augmented talents which people didn't even know they possessed. He hypnotised a policeman to believe he was Tchaikovsky—and now the man has entered the Conservatoire. Honest! Dr Kirilenko's method is a wonderful means of showing how every human being has such . . . such *capacities*."

Mikhail giggled; and Sonya hoped that her eyes hadn't shone—that would be *too* much.

"It isn't a matter of improving his acting talents *per se*," Felix said. "That isn't the idea, Dr Suslova. It's more a question of—"

"Of becoming Chekhov, to put it in a nutshell." Mikhail grinned at Sonya. "Ably assisted in this brave enterprise, I dearly hope, by you, my sweet little melon."

"What on earth do you mean, 'melon'?" she cried indignantly.

"Never fear! Just one of old Anton's jocular endearments. Addressed to lady friends who yearned for him in vain . . . He was a bit under-sexed, you see, so he preferred badinage to libido. Not that he didn't spend one well-documented night in the arms of Aphrodite! And he managed to fuck Olga Knipper when he finally married her. She had a miscarriage, so that proves it. But he wasn't exactly one of your hot lovers."

"*My* hot lovers? Really!"

"Infinite apologies! I guess I'm still a bit coarse to be a proper ascetic Anton, ain't I?"

22

"I don't know about ascetic!" said Felix. "He liked a booze-up now and then. And caviare and soft carpets." The Director rubbed his hands appreciatively.

"Hardly surprising," said Mikhail, "given all his ailments."

"Ah, but he *knew* what caused his ill health." Sergey wagged his tea about and spilled some. "Youthful poverty, and the fight for survival! But the Siberian journey rejuvenated him. Fresh air! And more important, a clear social goal."

"What a load of bunk." Mikhail winked at Sonya. "Let me tell you, my luscious cantaloupe, as far as politics was concerned I might as well have been living on Mars. Didn't I once define Socialism as a nervous disorder? Symptom: over-excitability? Though maybe it was *guilt* that sent me on my trip? Psychiatry knows all about guilt, eh?"

Sonya looked embarrassed, so Felix came to her aid.

"It's true enough that the critics were sniping at him for not seeming committed enough. All those 'Toads of the Inquisition'!"

Sergey glanced at the Director, meaningfully. 'Et tu, Felix?' his expression seemed to say.

Mikhail sniggered. "Actually, I'd say I was heading for a nervous breakdown back in '89. My brother Mikhail, snuffed it. Critics slamming me. *Ivanov*, a flop. My piles were right buggers. I was spitting blood."

Sonya hesitated. "So you prescribed a change of life for yourself?"

"Equally, I fancied myself as the Great Russian Novelist, didn't I? Sad, really. Me, the ultimate cameo artist. Hadn't the space in my head for a novel, had I? But off I went to Siberia searching for space. Not for literary copy, mark you. For infinity."

Felix nodded happily. "Yes: space. That's the ticket."

"And by experiencing space first hand, I purged myself of this fatuous ambition. How's that for a diagnosis, Doctor Suslova?"

Sonya shook her head non-committally.

"It was really daft of me to take on the infinite in Siberia. It just ain't possible to know the whole caboodle. Only idiots and humbugs tell you otherwise. Life's too foggy. Like my plays."

Felix clapped ironically. "Vintage stuff, Mike."

"Oh, come on," snapped Sergey. "You adopted a modern *scientific* approach in your plays. You believed in evidence. Life was your laboratory. So you wrote scientific drama and scientific fiction. Damn it, I mean *he* did! Chekhov did." Sergey sounded confused—uncertain as to whether he was addressing Mikhail Petrov or Anton Chekhov.

"My dear chap, you make me sound like Jules Verne. But I'll grant you one thing: I was a master of indeterminacy—if that's what you mean by modern science."

"Not by modern *Soviet* science! Nowadays we're much closer to knowing everything. It's only a question of time."

"Only fools and humbugs, I repeat!"

Fortunately they all heard the growl of a car labouring uphill; its wheels spun on the ice, but on it came. Once more, Sonya rushed to the window.

Victor Kirilenko was a burly gentle giant, with a puckish smile. His massive head was adorned with a bush of black curls, but his nose was thin and insignificant, with the result that his dark close deep-set eyes seemed to be burrowing together—to fuse perhaps into one cyclopean eye eventually. Under his charcoal suit he sported the biceps and chest of a muscle-builder; he looked as if he could hold chairs at arm's length for half an hour.

Osip had trailed into the room in Dr Kirilenko's wake, still carrying the Doctor's doffed overcoat with gloves stuffed in the pockets, as though to imply that this fellow was uncultured enough—compared with *artists*—to be keeping his coat on indoors. Osip peered down at Kirilenko's patent leather shoes for any trace of melting slush, then sniffed and wandered off.

"Honoured! It's very kind of you," Felix murmured. Gripping Kirilenko's hand deeply between thumb and forefinger, he thought to minimise the chance of having his own hand crushed. However, the handshake was soft and Kirilenko glanced down at Felix's deep grip in amusement.

24

"We are none of us what we seem, Felix Moseivich!" Only then did he relinquish Felix's hand. "In fact, we're all more than we seem. Much, much more! If that wretched taxi driver could have thought he was a great explorer, he'd have penetrated the mysteries of the route in a flash!" His eyes twinkled. "But I couldn't really risk hypnotising him, could I? Suppose a policeman stopped us and asked my driver his name, and he replied, 'Alexander Humboldt, at your service'! Dear me!"

"So there are perils involved in your theory of 'super-knowledge', eh?"

"No, no: 'Super*ability*' is the proper term. Any 'knowledge' has to come from the person in the trance. There's no point in persuading somebody that they're Leonardo or Levitan if they don't know a scrap about them. Whereas *you*," and Kirilenko fixed unerringly on Mikhail, "you know a good deal about Chekhov, eh?"

The actor toyed with his moustache. "That's as maybe . . . When you come down to brass tacks, we really haven't the foggiest about old Anton."

"In which case, it'll be up to *you* to select the true interpretation. And it'll be the true one because it'll be based upon your unconscious perceptions—those are a whole lot keener than your conscious faculties. Some people still find it hard to credit, but a trance isn't an *inferior* mental state. Not a bit of it! The encephalograph proves the contrary. A trance is actually a far more active mental state than ordinary waking life. So it's your 'super-perception' which we'll bring to the surface—recreating Chekhov in the process."

"Then *I* can polish off a decent script." Sergey stood up and shook hands. "I'm Gorodsky, by the way. It was I who spotted your stimulating piece in *Knowledge is Power*. So I drew it to the attention of Felix Moseivich. Of course, I'm fully aware of your line of work: what the popular journalists like to call 'Artificial Reincarnation'." A superior smile played across Sergey's lips. "You seem to have taken it a step further than most."

25

Kirilenko was aware of a certain edge in the man's voice. A writer wouldn't normally expect to take dictation from an actor—but in this instance a writer had taken steps to ensure this very thing! So was Mr Sergey Gorodsky entirely confident of his own creative ability? Or had he cleverly found the perfect pretext for exempting him from responsibility?

Actor Mikhail's bearing and tone seemed a lot more nonchalant. From the little he'd said so far, and from what Kirilenko had already heard about him, the man seemed devoid of artistic egotism. This Mikhail wasn't a star, with a star's personality, and prestige at stake. Excellent! In that case the superability channel wouldn't be blocked by competing signals . . .

"Well naturally Dr Kirilenko has gone a step further!" Sonya enthused. "You usually need a whole series of trances before the acquired skill filters through and stabilises. Usually the trance subject wakes up and promptly forgets all about being Tchaikovsky or whoever."

"Ah, so the subject forgets?" said Felix gaily. "Surely Mike isn't supposed to stay in a trance for weeks on end? How cruel to snap him out of it only when the film's in the can—and the poor fellow remembering nothing about his achievement! That wouldn't be art. It would be a conjuring trick."

Kirilenko scrutinised Levin's blithe countenance. How could the main point of the report in *Knowledge is Power* have so eluded the man? Kirilenko surmised that Levin was fantasizing him—as a blend of variety theatre strongman and stage mesmerist. Yes: here was The Stupendous Victor—stretched out between two chairs with a couple of blocks of concrete on his chest; and Sonya Suslova, clad in glittering attire, her thighs bare to the waist, would smash these with a sledge-hammer . . .

Levin's jocular tone said quite clearly: 'You, Doctor, might be able to direct anybody to become somebody else—scientifically. But I'm still the real Director. And if this film isn't fabulous, then you're a charlatan.'

'Ach, people's tangled, hidden motives! Sometimes,' thought

26

Kirilenko, 'I'm just too perceptive for my own good . . .' Yet danger was lurking here: danger to the Doctor's own reputation, which naturally he was hoping to propagandize by means of the proposed film for the sake of his research and future funding.

If Levin was maladroit in his handling of the film, or even mangled it subconsciously out of jealousy, the Doctor's hard-won reputation would be injured publicly on film screens through all the Republics . . .

It was clear that he, Kirilenko, was indeed being asked to perform as a stage hypnotist (all be it from the wings)—this was what Levin the impresario wanted. But Levin also demanded scientific credibility so that the film would be an advancement of human knowledge, something socially responsible. These were mixed motives.

"No, no!" Sonya protested. Sonya was an enthusiastic young lady but she wasn't entirely perceptive yet . . . "Dr Kirilenko has achieved a breakthrough in technique. From now on the trance subject can call up his alter ego at will. Just as an actor does," she added grandly, though the acting profession was a mystery to her. "The human mind isn't a single psychic system. It's many different systems, all co-operating. Like your own Film Unit!"

Mikhail smirked at Sergey, who looked upset.

"So Dr Kirilenko selectively hypnotises the left brain. But he leaves the other hemisphere semi-autonomous. This method he calls 'split-hypnosis'. Split-hypnosis should have important applications to the treatment of schizophrenia. But obviously it can help in the present case too, where . . . er . . . Mr Petrov is sane. And in all cases like it."

Kirilenko took over, charmingly. "That's why I'm so delighted to work with you. To be quite honest, I was thinking along these same lines myself. But you beat me to it, you smart fellows! And now, since I'm inexcusably late, perhaps we should proceed to a demonstration? The first course: the soup . . . When shall we begin with, Felix Moseivich?"

"When? Well, now . . ."

"No, I mean: which year?"

"Oh, hmm, yes. I see. What do you think, Sergey?"

"How about here in Krasnoyarsk? Just before Chekhov sets off for Kansk." Sergey thumbed through his notebook. "Let's see . . . that'll be . . . yes, May 29th 1890."

"I think," said Felix, "possibly we should slot in slightly earlier . . . just before Tomsk, hmm?"

Kirilenko drew an eye patch and an earplug out of his pocket.

Sergey shrugged. "It's all the same to me. Tomsk first, then we'll jump him forward to Krasnoyarsk."

"Fine," said Kirilenko. "Do we have a tape recorder? Yes . . . Paper? Good. Now, if you'll just kindly fix this patch comfortably over your right eye, Mikhail . . ."

Five

FLOODS! WATERY DESOLATION . . .

And a bittern, booming out its mad call like a pregnant cow mooing into an empty barrel.

Anton's felt boots were rotting apart, but he didn't dare subject his feet to the only alternative. The leather jackboots he had blithely equipped himself with were obviously an instrument of torture designed by the Spanish Inquisition to pinch and amputate one's pins.

Plodging knee-deep, he and the latest driver Yevgeny hauled another pair of neurotic, shying horses towards some huts on a little hill above the flood water. Anton's throat was hoarse from cursing, but this was the only form of encouragement these beasts understood.

In some places the swirling water was deep enough to drown a fellow. With so much mud churned up, though, there was no telling which places these were. Drizzle drifted down like a million grey spiders' silks. Presumably somewhere there was a proper river crossing. Somewhere.

A tall peasant woman emerged from one of the houses. This was a heavy mud and clay edifice with a thatched timber roof. Two other such huts stood off from it, and together with a row of byres these formed a courtyard with litter and tackle lying about. An upturned sledge rested against a wagon. The place seemed relatively prosperous.

From the porch, the woman hailed them. "Are you the medical assistant?"

"We're lost!" Yevgeny howled back at her. Opening his mouth

29

wide, the more to magnify their misfortunes, he afforded Anton an eyeful of gums awash with pus due to pyorrhoea.

"But I *am* a doctor!" shouted Anton.

They tramped on to a slope of gluey black muck, which admittedly would grow splendid crops. A few more loud oaths, and the horses were out of the water too, dragging the skidding cart which was Yevgeny's pride and joy.

"I'm going to Tomsk," Anton told the woman.

"It's God's will! He guided you here."

"Ay, and who'll guide us away again?" demanded Yevgeny.

"Oh, our Boris'll do that. Just as soon as . . ."

Oh yes. Just as soon as his Honour, the Doctor, cures septic appendicitis or cancer of the spleen or something else equally daunting. Anton felt heavy chains settle upon him. With as good a grace as he could muster he submitted and followed the woman indoors.

Grandpa lay abed on top of the stove. Four or five kids peered out from a deep and fuggy shelf slung beneath the ceiling. Three crones, who bore a remarkable resemblance to the Witches in *Macbeth*, were huddled round a wooden chest—the parental bed. A sick woman lay moaning on it. A hairy bull of a man stood about, twiddling his thumbs and sighing. A spindly youth, who looked as if he had gone for height in the style of an overcrowded seedling, sat slumped on a bench staring morosely at his reflection in the blade of a knife. And there was Grandma, clucking away like an old hen, with Baby swaddled in her lap. The place was disgracefully overcrowded.

On closer inspection, Grandma wasn't actually clucking. Her toothless gums were smacking away at an impromptu dummy: a twist of cloth with a bread crust in it, or if Baby was specially lucky some bacon rind. Baby in its mummy cloth was all open mouth and wide liquid eyes. As Anton approached, Grandma quickly popped the saliva-sodden nib into Baby's mouth. Arms bound by its sides, mouth stoppered, Baby now only had his eyes to talk to the world with.

Anton had given up trying to count the number of people in this room. What was the use? He could hardly turf them out into the drizzle. Anyway, they probably wouldn't go. Why should they? Here was a grand tale unfolding: of sickness and a stranger.

He jerked his thumb in the direction of the chest-bed.

"What's wrong with her?" he asked the tall woman.

"Well, you see, Sir, she had her baby. But it died, and a bit of the afterbirth's stuck in her. So Pelagaya Osipovna tried to pull it out."

"She tried to pull it out? *What with*?"

The tall woman searched around and produced a lamp hook, rusty and sooty, with blood stains on it.

Oh shit. Unbelievable! They may as well have murdered the poor bitch! Yes, using the same damn knife that scarecrow of a youth was holding! He must be the husband . . . And quite conceivably they *had* been planning to use that insanitary blade as their next surgical instrument.

With an effort Anton controlled his feelings. It was all perfectly comprehensible. Anything other than this ignorant butchery would be the miracle . . .

"Yevgeny," he shouted. "Get me my doctor's bag!"

While he waited, he began searching his pockets in a quiet fury, he knew not quite for what. The woman would die—no doubt of it. Whatever he did.

His fingers encountered folded paper and he pulled this out. Oh yes, that sheet of bum-wiper from the post station. He hadn't even used it. Unfolding the torn scrap of *Siberian Herald*, he stared glazedly at the contents as if he was consulting a pamphlet on gynaecology which he just happened to have on hand.

> . . . in the North-West the peasants ob-
> served racing through the sky a shining
> body in the shape of a cylinder, too bright
> to behold. Moments later a huge cloud of
> black smoke arose and a tongue of flame

shot up into the heavens. A crashing noise, as of artillery, was heard several times. The ground itself shook, throwing many people down, and horses even fell to their knees. A hot fierce wind blew up suddenly, tearing the roof from one house. Many people cried out in terror that this was the end of the world.

There is no doubt whatever that a large heavenly body must have crashed to earth somewhere; though where exactly is less certain . . .

This scrap of newspaper was dated . . . 2nd of July 1888. A year and ten months ago.

Hysteria, wild exaggeration, ignorance! Anton could have moaned aloud.

But the sick woman was already doing that, while she lay corrupting internally. Stuffing the paper back into his pocket, resolved that he definitely would wipe his arse on such nonsense as soon as he had time, Anton stepped over to the victim. He pulled the covers back to inspect the bloody atrocity underneath. The kids stared down from the rafters, goggle-eyed; and the crones crooned softly.

Six

Krasnoyarsk
May 29th, 1890

How are you, Olga, my precious star-gazer?

Here am I in Siberia, and you're far away. But how I wish you had been at my side last night so that I could squeeze your hand in the starlight and ask your advice on matters interplanetary, of which a humble doctor and scribbler knows little. (Other than that the cosmos is vast and drear, and that time stretches out intolerably till this planet will be as cold as space itself . . .)

But first a scribbler ought to set the scene, don't you think?

Krasnoyarsk is an excellent town—particularly after such vile Asiatic holes as Tomsk. Goodness alone knows why they send exiles here to Krasnoyarsk! This must seem more like a reward, what with the grand forested mountains encompassing the city like high walls, and the broad swift Yenisey winding its way through—worthier of Levitan's brush even than the Volga. And I mustn't forget the town itself. Why, there are paved streets and gracious churches and handsome houses built of stone! But they do send exiles here, and they've done so for years. Result? Krasnoyarsk is quite cultured, as well as being picturesque.

Anyhow, I have fallen in with an army doctor and a pair of lieutenants all on their way to the Amur. We intend to travel onward together, so I shall hardly need my revolver. Boldly would I harrow Hell itself in company with this trio.

Can you read my writing? This ink is disgusting. Blot and splotch.

So let me tell you about these brave fellows. Dr Rodé is something of a philosopher and pessimist—and, by turns, an idealist. Half the time he speaks of the new and happy life awaiting us in some distant future epoch when we'll all fly across Siberia by balloon, and when a sixth sense will be developed so that our minds can reach out to the stars. Then he grows gloomy (worn out by his enthusiasm) and it's all a case of: 'We can't be real. The present can't be real. This is all a nightmare in somebody's mind a thousand years ahead!'

Then there's Baron Nikolai Vershinin. The Baron really puts it on as a military man, growling the letter 'R' deep in this throat like the doyen of some posh cavalry regiment. He's forever barking at people. You'd think he was ordering a Cossack to be flogged for cowardice when he calls for a cup of tea and some jam. Generally he's abusive in company that he doesn't know, but just you get him on his own and he's quite a kindly, sensible man—with a concern for society. 'The avalanche is coming,' he'll warn you. He thinks Science might save us, though. And he has read Herbert Spencer, or at least he says so. But he does throw his weight around; and there's quite a lot of weight to throw.

Lastly there's Vasily Fedotik, who never glances at any reading matter except a newspaper. I'm sure he hasn't lifted an intellectual finger for the last twenty years. All that interests our Fedotik is hunting and boozing, and once he has made up his mind on a subject it would be far too much trouble to alter his opinion. One thing he has fixed in his mind is that Rodé and Vershinin are both excellent wise fellows, so he has a habit of dropping the most droll *aperçus* into the conversation, which are all warped echoes of something the other two men have said. Invariably these 'mottos' are way off beam, like the wisdom of a senile babushka.

Yesterday evening, out I sallied in company with these three musketeers to see the town . . .

Everything on the journey so far has turned out contrary to expectation. In Tomsk where the local ladies are as charming as a butt of frozen herrings—fit mates for a walrus—who would have imagined that the Assistant Chief of Police would be a connoisseur of my works? Who would have expected him to do me the honour of driving me on a tour of the local houses of prostitution, as his way of paying respect to my literary achievements?

Anvhow, there was I forming a wholly favourable impression of the town on our promenade around its remarkably clean streets—when Fedotik must suffer a sudden attack of drought. So we all had to perform an about-turn into the less salubrious quarter of town to find him an inn on the double for medicinal comfort. Oh ho, thought I: Tomsk revisited!

"This fatal attraction for low life!" proclaimed the good Dr Rodé, as we hastened towards the dives. "It proves how democratic we Russians are."

"Quite right," said Fedotik. "The Prince shall sit down with the pauper."

"Probably the Prince *is* a pauper," observed the Baron, with a raucous laugh.

"That's because there are too many Princes and Counts, and Barons if you'll pardon me," said Rodé. "Yet who's to say that's such a bad thing? In the future everybody may be ennobled."

Vershinin nodded. "Ennobled by the progress of Science. One chap'll be a Count of Chemistry, and another a Duke of Dentistry."

"Trouble with all these intellectual chappies," said Fedotik, "is they have their heads stuck in the clouds." And he remembered to add, "Present company excepted."

"That's when we Russians feel most at home," Rodé said. "With our heads stuck in the clouds. And why should that be? Is it because ordinary life's so stuck in the mud? Is it because we're all just stuck in a bad dream, anyway?"

Fedotik appears to possess a sixth sense for inns; quite soon we found a fairly decent one. Decent, if you overlooked the blue fug of wood smoke proceeding from the stove . . .

We ordered ourselves a bottle of Smirnov Twenty-One (would you believe?) and drank a toast to the next stage of the journey.

Sitting nearby there was a man whose face was as flabby as a boiled turnip. From time to time he buttoned up his coat resolutely then unbuttoned it again in a perfect mime of frustration—as though he ought to set out on some trip but was unable to make up his mind. Every time this occurred he edged a little closer to us, trying to eavesdrop on our conversation in the usual manner of inebriates, the better to butt in.

His opportunity arose when Rodé said something or other to me, 'speaking as one man of science to another . . .'

"Excuse me, Gentlemen," interrupted our turnip, "But Science is the most noble and beautiful pursuit!" His voice had a sanctimonious lilt, with undertones of wheedling recrimination. "Excuse me, but in my opinion your scientist struggles with Nature—out of love of Mankind!"

Our Russian genius for soulful generalizations . . .

"Quite right," agreed Fedotik. "Nature, red in tooth and claw, has to be tamed by the brave hunter!" He poured himself another glassful.

Vershinin went bright red in the face. "Who the Devil do you think you are?"

"Sidorov, by your leave. Ilya Alexandrovich."

"Be off with you, you banal Sidorov! How could a Sidorov know one iota of the heights of human thought?"

Naturally Sidorov shuffled himself even closer to us.

"Excuse me, Gentlemen, but banality is the whole trouble— you've hit the nail on the head. The ordinary human being is downright stupid. You can see that easily in these God-forsaken Siberian holes."

"Present premises excepted," chipped in Fedotik.

"But Nature is even stupider. The Earth whirls round the Sun like a child's spinning top: how trivial it all is! At any moment a dark star or a wandering moon might crash into us. Splat! And that's that. Goodbye to the Parthenon and to Venice *Serenissima*." Tears rose to Sidorov's eyes. "Look at your average Siberian—a beast, isn't he? Mind you, he's your ordinary run of Russian peasant who's been brutalised."

"A brute needs the whip," quoted Fedotik.

"Mark my words, Sirs, compared with *him* the tribes a few hundred versts north of here are noble . . .," and Sidorov hunted for the word, "savages. Well, almost. Compared to him they're quite magnificent. They're heroes. But how can they be heroes if they've always stayed here?—that's what puzzles me. They never rose above their condition. Whereas we local Russians have sunk down to it. Ah, the disgusting flatness of it all! And under the surface everything is rotten and decayed . . . What was I talking about?"

At this moment the wick in the nearest lamp began to hum loudly. Sidorov pricked up his ears as though he heard something rush through the sky above the roofs of Krasnoyarsk. He buttoned his coat swiftly and ran out of the inn, leaving the door wide open. Thus we were able to see him standing in the street, staring up at the night sky as if to confirm that all the stars were in their proper places. Or perhaps he was only wondering whether it was going to rain, since his boots had holes in them. Presently he returned, unbuttoned and subsided right up against us.

"Excuse me, but I'm sacrificing myself to Science," he confided to me in a loud whisper. (I swear to you, Olga—by Mars and Jupiter—that I am *not* inventing this Sidorov as a mirror for my own soul!) "Why, if I went to Moscow to present a proper report to the authorities, they'd make me a Professor or even a Privy Councillor on the spot. You have the flavour of Moscow about you, Sir, isn't it so?"

Reluctantly I conceded the fact.

Vershinin dug Fedotik in the ribs. "We've caught ourselves a provincial bore. Set the dogs on him, Vasily Romanych!"

"Ah Moscow!" cried Sidorov, in tipsy torment. "Freedom, fulfilment! Afterwards I could drain the bog-land. With all the trees down, I could sell the timber and plant grain. Alas, it's too cold for that . . . Anyway, the mosquitoes! And the people: too corrupted. Maybe you two men of Science might help me present a proper report?"

37

As soon as these words were out, to my no very great surprise Sidorov became jealously hostile.

"Scientists! Your ordinary scientists!" he sneered. "If the Earth blew up tomorrow they'd go on staring down their microscopes like England's Lord Nelson."

"Turning a blind eye," Fedotik dutifully supplied.

"Would they listen to me? As for the authorities . . . well, that's our whole sickness, isn't it? Authority: how we worship authority! Ah, I can see how you despise me for not acting like a hero and setting off forthwith for Moscow and fame . . . But it isn't so easy. There aren't any authorities on an event like this—except for the Bible narrative of the Cities of the Plain, devastated by God. I can't persuade anybody in Krasnoyarsk to do anything about it. In Moscow, who cares about Krasnoyarsk?"

By now Baron Nikolai was in a transport of wrath. He grabbed Sidorov by the lapels. "What the Devil are you talking about?" he shouted into the man's face.

Our turnip was shaken, but all the drink he had swilled gave him courage.

"You smart Muscovites haven't even heard! And it's the greatest mystery of the age."

"If you don't tell me, I swear I'll beat you to a pulp!"

"The explosion that devastated the taiga. The visitor from space. You haven't heard."

"Hang on," said I . . .

Because, my celestial charmer, I *had* heard of it—had you? I refer to the enclosed clipping from the *Siberian Herald*, which I originally intended for quite another, 'hygienic', purpose.

Sidorov went on to spin us the tallest tale I'd ever heard, of huge destruction a few hundred versts north of Krasnoyarsk up by the Stony Tunguska River. I shall list his 'details' in a moment, since I want to ask you quite seriously, Olga: What do you make of all this? My telescopic tormentress, I request your frank scientific opinion . . .

38

Seven

A YOUNG WORKMAN was plucking idly at a guitar, and singing to himself. A beefy-faced fellow at the next table ordered a plate of meat croquettes. And Fedotik called out for another bottle of Smirnov Twenty-One.

In a moment of panic about the mounting bill, Anton clutched at his stomach. This was a reflex he really must put a stop to! Where else could his money belt be? It could hardly unbuckle itself and slide down his trouser leg.

"Hungry?" enquired Fedotik.

"No, I just felt as if . . . That's to say . . ." Anton shook his head.

"It's easy enough to pick up bugs—nothing to be ashamed of," remarked Sidorov.

Vershinin eyed Sidorov sourly. "We're all of us bugs on the backside of the world—some more than others, eh?"

Since his purchase of the springless carriage back in Tomsk, Anton's money belt was lighter by a hundred and thirty roubles. If this rattletrap got wrecked before he reached Irkutsk, or if he couldn't sell it there, then he'd be smashed . . . Everything cost twice as much as he'd bargained for. He still owed Suvorin fifteen hundred roubles, to be paid off partly by writing travelogues. The trouble was, journalism was like trying to squeeze juice out of fleas' genitals! What on earth could he write about in the next one?

Perhaps the problem had already solved itself. Rolling another cigarette, he listened avidly to Sidorov's tale of cosmic catastrophe . . .

*

"A hundred million trees, felled all at once! Everything trembled and shook. Fountains of water gushed from the ground, so they say. A hurricane roared through Kansk, and a tidal wave raced up the Yenisey. The night sky stayed bright for weeks—don't ask me why! And whole herds of reindeer were incinerated on the spot. Others got scabs all over them—"

"What sort of scabs?"

But Vershinin had lost patience. "Oh, turn the tap off. The world's mad for putting up with the likes of you. No wonder it gives a shrug now and then."

"No, hang on," said Anton. "This happened around Midsummer '88, right?"

As he recalled, he had been at Lintvareva's summer place at the time. Old Pleshcheyev had been there too, forever burning incense to himself—just as if the grand old man was some holy icon. His cigar fumes gave everyone else a headache. So the party often strolled out into the park to clear their heads, even at midnight. And it had been so *bright*. Astonishingly bright. All night long—brighter than any moonlight. Everyone had remarked on it at the time . . .

"If our celestial visitor had exploded on top of Petersburg, surely this would have spoken to our society! But what can it tell us here—that God is angry with the taiga? It tells us nothing at all. So nothing has changed . . . It's too much for me, Sir! I can adapt to ten trees falling down—but a hundred million? No, it's a joke. And nothing happens, nothing alters. We could have a revolution and nothing would change. Ever. Ever. Ever!"

"I don't know about *that*," growled Vershinin.

"Such an immense event—and it failed to kill a single person. So far as I know. That's the kind of country we're trapped in. Much better if it *had* killed a hundred or a thousand people! Then somebody might take a closer look, and the condition of the Siberian people might alter." Sidorov held two trembling fingers a little way apart. "By this much. But where did it have to happen? Exactly where it was guaranteed to be ignored by everybody. So it's all a joke. What does it matter if a comet strikes the Earth?"

Once more Sidorov leapt up, buttoned himself and repaired to the door to stand staring up into the starry void.

Anton thought sadly: 'Our turnip's seeing some decoration being pinned to his breast, far away in Moscow. Yes, a jewelled star third class, to honour the reporter of a fallen star! As he stares up into the firmament, somewhere out there in infinite space fame awaits him . . .'

The man returned, slumped down and groaned.

"I'm missing my chance—all for the want of a few hundred roubles . . . I really ought to get up an expedition, don't you see? Not one of your dilettante outings, but a real scientific expedition equipped with a theodolite and stuff. *Moscow's* the starting point for that. No one's interested here—they've all forgotten. But how can I go to Moscow without good evidence? And how can I get good evidence till after I've been to Moscow? I appeal to you, Gentlemen, will you lend me ten roubles?"

"Aha!" exclaimed Vershinin. "Now we see him in his true colours."

Dr Rodé smiled wanly. "Gentlemen, perhaps a small experiment might be conducted at this juncture, to discover scientifically what this poor wretch will do with the money? Will it be Smirnov vodka, do you suppose? Or Koshelev? We could bet on the outcome—the loser pays the bill."

"Here, have some anyway." In an apparent fit of bonhomie Fedotik slopped a few fingers of vodka into an empty glass. "Go on: a man needs a drink." But then he teased the glass towards Sidorov, as though he might hook it back again.

Like a cat pouncing on a pigeon, Sidorov snatched the glass and drank. Abruptly he began to cry, his tears diluting the remaining spirit.

"How can I visit Tunguska till I'm able to raise an expedition? How can I raise an expedition without going there first, to prove the need for one?"

Fedotik nodded sagely. "Those indeed are the horns of his dilemma."

"I've only spoken to people who have in turn spoken to eye witnesses. You have to discount a lot, sometimes. These people talk of giant rats, the size of cows, that burrow underground. You and I, Sirs, know that those are the corpses of mammoths frozen in the undersoil . . . But the trees, ah the trees! A hundred million laid low in an instant. What have logic and morality to do with that? It's an accidental circumstance, Sirs. We come into our life by accident. We often leave it by accident. In between is a chapter of accidents."

Fedotik nudged Vershinin. "No doubt about it, he's a Superfluous Man."

"And it's all as nothing to this endless earthly monster: our own country. She swallows the incident as a cow swallows a fly. How true that disaster strikes where nobody sees or hears it! In the circumstances, happiness is quite impossible."

"A Superfluous Man," repeated Fedotik, delighted with this insight.

"Does it matter if a comet strikes the Earth? Yet for it to happen, and *be ignored*—because the only people who can think are three thousand versts away—it's a joke that passes endurance. And there's an even greater joke . . . If this hadn't happened in the back of beyond, if it had struck Petersburg full in the face—chastising that rich, uncaring city!—in that case the whole world would have known. But I—! But I—!"

"You would have been nobody, then," Anton said gently. "You would have had nothing."

Sidorov stared at him blearily. "So you do understand? You're my true brother."

Doubtless, reflected Anton, they were brothers—in dishevelment. His own coat stank of tar, and Sidorov's coat was equally filthy. Their boots were a disgrace. Anton tipped back his head, abstracting himself.

Here was an interesting case indeed. The man had been taken

over by an event, which hadn't *quite* dropped into his lap. He had been presented—from outer space, would you believe?—with a grand ambition. In another man's case this might have been an obsessive desire to retire to a farm and grow his own gooseberries or something. But in this instance *desolation* commanded him— and he could no more leave this part of Siberia than a prospector in the Yukon could desert the rumour of the Motherlode. Presumably his life could only go downhill from here . . .

Suppose Sidorov did raise the wherewithal to travel to Moscow? What could he possibly show to anybody there? All those tumbled trees he spoke of were unknown except to the migrating birds, which alone knew the scale of this land . . . and to a few tribesmen who didn't exist within Russian society.

"Obsession," Anton said softly, as if it was the title of a tale yet unwritten.

Fedotik heard him. "Once a man's obsessed, there's nothing you can do about it! Take my word for it." He cocked an imaginary gun at the ceiling. "Bang, bang, down they come." He laughed guilelessly.

And yet, thought Anton . . . What if it were all true? What if one of the greatest mysteries in the history of the world really had happened not so far from here? But no one was paying attention . . . It was as though the Crucifixion took place, and everybody was away in the country.

"I may as well be a convict in exile," went on Sidorov gloomily. "Siberia isn't a real place. It's so much stuffing in between the Urals and the Pacific. Yet how petty my crimes are—compared with the taiga! And how petty everything is . . ." Ineptly he fumbled with his coat buttons.

Anton reached out and touched the suffering man on the arm.

"Look, Ilya Alexandrovich, I just happen to be writing a series of articles for *New Times* in Moscow—"

At that very moment a loud *twang* sounded through the room—as though some cosmic clock had chimed in the inn, or as if time itself had suddenly snapped in two. Briefly the room fell silent, till the note had died away.

"Sod it!" swore the guitar player, one of whose strings had snapped.

"That's right, *New Times*," Anton said excitedly.

Eight

FELIX COULD NO longer contain himself. "Dear boy, what are you *saying*? Bring him out of the trance!"

A worried Dr Kirilenko complied. The tape recorder was switched off and notepads were laid aside.

For a moment or two Mikhail blinked in bewilderment, newly restored to himself. As he took in the room and its frumpy furnishings with contemporary eyes, he grinned. But a puzzled look crossed his face as he registered the expressions of the others in the room, and began to recall . . .

"It's like waking up from a dream," he muttered. "A dream that tries to fade away. If you concentrate, you can remember."

"You'll soon establish perfect control," said Sonya soothingly. "You'll soon have a sense of conscious continuity between yourself—and your other self."

"I was in that joint just off Karl-Marx Street! I'm sure it's the same place . . . This room was the inn. And before—no, afterwards, I'm getting mixed up—I was in a hotel room. Now what was I doing? Got it! I was penning a letter to Olga Kundasova . . ."

"And there it is." Sonya indicated the notepad lying open on the sofa beside him; the pages were covered with scrawly handwriting.

Sergey launched himself across the room to snatch up the pad. "It's a bloody *mélange*, that's what this is! These officer fellows are straight out of *Three Sisters*—names and all. Okay, so Chekhov did travel part of the way with an army doctor and a couple of soldiers. But all this nonsense about the comet! Little did I suspect, Petrov, when you made that crack about Jules Verne—!" He tossed the notepad down.

Felix also stood up, so as not to be dominated by Sergey. "Let's get our facts straight. *Something* exploded over Tunguska in the middle of Siberia in 1910, right?"

"Wrong," said Sergey. "It was 1908. I once wrote an article on the Tunguska mystery."

"I stand corrected. Anyway, Anton Chekhov was safely in his grave by then. It certainly didn't happen in 1888, dear boy!"

Kirilenko stood up too. "Excuse me, Felix Moseivich, but I am safe in presuming that Mikhail is fully *au courant* with the actual life of Chekhov?"

"Absolutely. Must we all keep breaking out in French? We're Soviet artists, not nineteenth century Russians."

"If there are *no* gaps in Mikhail's knowledge of the facts, then he couldn't possibly invent something to fill those gaps."

"He could hardly fill gaps, if there aren't any."

"So he's fantasizing," Sergey said.

"But he can't be. Oh, admittedly he fantasizes that he's Chekhov—in the psychological sense. But he has to do so *accurately*, just as I instructed him to. He can only invent around the known facts. He doesn't have free rein to make up whatever he chooses. I must say, nothing like this has happened before in my experience. It's an important and fascinating new development." However, Kirilenko hardly sounded very happy about it. Actually, what had happened was confoundedly embarrassing . . .

"Maybe Petrov's insane?" suggested Sergey. "You know: cuckoo? Round the twist?"

"Thanks," said Mikhail.

"We have to get to the bottom of this," said Kirilenko. "I shall reinforce my instructions—then we'll skip forward a few weeks. Probably that'll put us back on the right track . . ."

Just then the double doors opened and Osip wandered into the room without having troubled to knock—attracted by their voices raised in dispute?

"Damn it, man!" snapped Felix. Was the caretaker keeping watch on them, as well as on the building?

"Would you lot like something to eat?" asked Osip. "Some refreshments?"

Felix fixed him with a hard stare for several moments, before allowing, "Maybe we should break for lunch."

"It couldn't have been a comet, could it?" Sonya said. "The Tunguska thing? I thought it had all the characteristics of a nuclear explosion in mid-air? The heat flash. Radiation scabs on the reindeer. The pattern of tree-fall, the growth spurt in the trees afterwards . . ."

"Oh yes," agreed Sergey sarcastically. "Naturally I came to that conclusion in my article. A nuclear explosion in 1908—nothing more obvious, when you come to think of it."

Felix noted how Osip had pricked up his ears. "Be off with you," he told the caretaker. "Get on with it—we're hungry."

Slowly Osip slouched from the room.

"There's no other explanation, is there, that fits all the facts?" said Sonya.

"Soviet scientists are working hard on the Tunguska problem every year," Sergey explained. "They use helicopters and geiger counters."

"And still nobody knows for sure," said Felix. "From all I've heard it's . . . damn it, it's downright Chekhovian! Who knows what happened? Who'll ever know?"

"It was *you* who dragged outer space into all this, in the first place!" Sergey shouted accusingly.

Outside, the sun shone down dazzlingly upon the snowscape, though a curtain of cloud was in the offing . . .

Nine

ANTON GAZED ACROSS a grim river, the colour of slate. Barges drifted by with dozens of boatmen lining their gunwales, clutching poles like medieval soldiers armed with pikes. It was hellishly cold.

If he could only get over to the other side! But the bargees only pulled rude faces at him and shouted abuse.

He fled from the riverbank, pursued by their taunts, and immediately came upon a cemetery. The stone gate posts were crumbling, as were the tombs within; yet a funeral procession had just arrived, and filed inside. The mourners seemed to comprise everyone he had ever known. Suvorin was there. So was Pleshcheyev. Olga Kundasova, too—and Nikolai Leikin. Modest Tchaikovsky stood next to Maria Kiseleva. Levitan, Evgenia, Masha . . . And without exception everyone was weeping unconsolably.

Anton rushed into the cemetery to try to explain that the coffin was full of stones. But the mocking laughter of the bargees still rang in his ears, confusing him. Those evil fellows were still watching him from somewhere—openly and contemptuously like police spies . . .

He woke up with a start—and the majestic Yenisey lay before him, in full flood, rather than that Styx of his dreams. A stalwart ferry was ploughing against the fierce current, ever nearer to the shore, to bear him back to Krasnoyarsk. Horses stamped fretfully; harness jingled.

"Ever thought you were being watched, Ilya?" he asked Sidorov, who was holding the reins. "You know the feeling? The

48

old animal sense, as if something's boring between your shoulder blades?"

"Uh." Sidorov made a feeble attempt to shake himself out of his stupor.

"I ought to be in Sakhalin now, taking a census. And something's driving me down a different road—like a bayonet sticking in my back. I must be sick in my mind. A psychopath, eh?"

"Uh."

And there it was! Not insanity, but *fatigue*. Exhaustion was the cause of his dream and source of his mental confusion. Neurasthenia reached unique new depths on any Siberian journey—but especially on a trip through the endless forests of the taiga. Time stopped entirely. One's brain clogged up.

"Uh huh." Sidorov's face was so grimy that he might have been masquerading as a Negro, smeared with boot polish.

Anton rubbed his own face. His knuckles came away black as a lamp wick. Whenever Summer lightning struck the forests, fires dragged sooty palls across the Road. Which was worse: the floods and gluey mud before—or this dry dusty smoking heat? Both were vile . . . And no matter how many trees were burned to a cinder, it never seemed to diminish by one jot the endless ranks of pines reeking of resin, of larches and firs, and those gloomy birches which were darker than the birches of Russia, less sentimental in hue . . .

"My God, if a jaunt of three hundred versts to Kansk and back knocks a fellow up like this—that's on a road, mind you!—Heaven help us once we're off the beaten track!"

"Don't worry, Anton Pavlovich." Sidorov had come alive again. "Wherever Man exists, there are tracks. The Tungusi know where the paths are . . . One day, I swear to you, this forest will be driven back—oh, maybe as far as Kansk itself! You'll see fields of cabbages and potatoes. And the one thing which will bring that day closer is to call attention to Siberia!"

"You know, back in Russia I used to think the crash of an axe was such a cruel sound . . ."

49

"We're all of us lost in a dark wood, blundering around. We need to let a little light in. Don't we?"

"Yes."

"Really, our problem's just one of timing—as our surveyor friend says. We could hop in a boat right away. The Yenisey would carry us off to the North without us lifting a finger. But as soon as we left the river . . ."

"'Ay, there's the rub,' as Vasily Fedotik would say."

"This taiga's evil, Anton Pavlovich. The mosquitoes can eat you alive. Horses can drown in the devilish bogs."

"So we wait till it freezes—then the Winter swallows us. It's madness. Besides, have you considered the cost?"

How slowly yet valiantly the ferry moved . . . A group of peasants shared the jetty with them, perching on baskets of spring onions. A circuit judge sat pompously upon his carriage. Anton's thoughts drifted back over the strange chain of events of the past few weeks . . .

Commencing with his visit to the offices of the *Krasnoyarets* newspaper on the morning after he had first heard Sidorov tell his tale . . . The editor insisted on holding a reception in Anton's honour at his own home that very evening. Present at that soirée had been a fairly fatuous company of ladies, drummed up in haste, who oo-ed and ah-ed over him and tinkled pianos and recited Pushkin—and the not-so-fatuous Countess Lydia Zelenina who was playing it up as a 'romantic exile . . .'

There Anton had also met a Czech surveyor, Jaroslav Mirek by name, who had something to do with a scheme for building a railway, but who was kicking his heels in Krasnoyarsk.

One thing had led to another, which had led in turn to a third, till a fortnight later Anton was still becalmed in Krasnoyarsk—as were Vershinin, Rodé and Fedotik. It now transpired that the three musketeers were in reality stuck for funds, having extravagantly run through their allowances of two thousand roubles apiece. But by then Vershinin was talking brashly of persuading the Governor to second him from his assignment on the Amur,

50

'for a real adventure', while Ilya Sidorov who had stopped behaving quite so superfluously, was all for hauling Anton off to Kansk on a fact-finding investigation—a trip from which they were only now returning . . .

Fate, it seemed, had conspired. Yet what of the convicts and their women and children still languishing all this while in Sakhalin? Could it be that there was more than one way to pay one's dues to Science?

Presently the ferry grounded against the jetty. Ropes were tossed ashore, and the judge's driver flicked his whip, catching a peasant across the rump.

Dismounting, Anton and Sidorov hauled their own team and carriage out upon this mighty warrior of rivers.

Once he was back in the hotel on Blagoryeshtchenskaya Anton promptly drank five glasses of tea in a row till his face glowed as red as a beetroot—and sorted through his accumulated correspondence. Those troikas of the Imperial Postal Service might run you down without a second thought, but they did deliver the goods at wonderful speed.

His article about the 'Tunguska Mystery' was already in print in *New Times*; already it had caused a bit of a sensation in the newspapers, so Suvorin reported—there was even talk of raising a fund.

Apart from Suvorin's epistle there were letters from sister Mariya—blessedly accompanying a packet of decent tobacco, to spare him from the Siberian variety which resembled pounded hay—and from mother Evgenia, also from Pleshcheyev. Then there was a long reply to his own appeal for scientific advice, from Olga Kundasova; and finally there was a bulky letter from some complete stranger who lived in Borovsk, fourscore versts to the south of Moscow.

He read the family news first while guzzling the fourth and fifth cups of tea and enjoying a real Ukrainian smoke; then opened the lady astronomer's letter.

51

This was full of astronomical speculations about comets and meteors and meteorites and bolides and the craters on the Moon. From it he gathered that there ought to be a huge crater hidden somewhere out in the taiga, with a fortune in iron and nickel and platinum buried underneath. A fortune, that is, for any passing reindeer or Tungusi tribesman enterprising enough to build a mine and smelting works and a railway line . . .

Anton was beginning to itch all over as the heat from the tea tried to sweat its way out through his blocked pores. Putting aside the letter from Borovsk till later, he hurried out to pay a call on the public bath house. On the way he fell in with Jaroslav Mirek, heading for the same destination, though the Czech was hardly one tenth as filthy as Anton.

To Anton's embarrassment the water turned first to brown then to inky black, as the two men soaped and scrubbed and ducked. To take their attention off the dirt, Anton went into Kundasova's notions of meteoric wealth in lavish detail.

"Hmm," said Mirek. He was a short, hairy, muscular man with keen blue eyes. "If that's so, it's just what this part of the world needs. Yet what incredible difficulties . . . It might be fifty years before we could even contemplate utilisation."

'Utilisation' was one of Mirek's favourite words. He habitually saw the trees of the taiga as nothing more than so many railway sleepers planted upright in the ground, waiting to be pushed over and trimmed.

"Maybe it needs a change in the system of government, too," he added quietly. "But that's no business of mine."

They repaired to the steam room together, where they thrashed each other with birch besoms; after which Anton felt ravenous.

He dined alone back at the hotel, in the restaurant, on boiled eggs with cream followed by flabby boiled chicken and cabbage. Afterwards he went up to his room and poured himself a generous glass of spirits; then he opened the letter from Borovsk . . .

Most Truly Honoured Sir,

Permit me to introduce myself. My name is Konstantin Eduardovich Tsiolkovsky, and currently I am employed as a teacher of arithmetic and geometry at the elementary school here in Borovsk . . .

'What's this, then? An application for a job?' Quickly Anton skimmed through the long letter, various passages catching his eye.

. . . my sincere hope is that next year may see the publication of my paper on *How to Protect Fragile & Delicate Objects from Jolts & Shocks*—with special reference to gravitational acceleration due to interplanetary travel . . .

. . . my own humble, and as yet unpublished essay in the art of fiction—of a species which might perhaps best be described as 'Science Fantasy'—entitled *On the Moon* . . .

'Science Fantasy, eh? What's that?' wondered Anton. 'A new school of literature? A sort of Odoyevsky and Jules Verne thing? Aha, now I see, this fellow wants me to recommend him to a publisher!'

But surely no one in their right mind would despatch a letter thousands of versts for that reason alone? Not unless they were crackers . . .

. . . ballistic shockwave . . .

Anton skipped through to the end.

. . . therefore my conclusion, most respected Anton Pavlovich, based upon the newspaper reports from Siberia which you quote in your article, together with the other hearsay evidence you cite, is that an interplanetary space vehicle—perhaps from the planet Mars—exploded high above the forests of the taiga whilst attempting to enter the Earth's atmosphere subsequent to its journey through the void. This disaster would have been

53

caused by overheating, due to the resistance and friction of gas molecules encountered at high speed.

I have carried out some experiments, employing matchsticks for trees, and I feel confident in predicting that the trees directly beneath the centre of the explosion will be found to remain erect, although stripped of their foliage and branches.

I have also carried out some calculations, a copy of which I append to this letter. I have always felt sure, hitherto, that a 'ship of space' such as I envisage ought to be powered by a principle of 'jet propulsion' employing liquid fuel as the propellant. However, I have estimated the probable size of this 'ship', basing my estimate on the appearance of the shockwave in the upper atmosphere, as described by your good self. And I have carefully calculated the explosive force of appropriate masses of various propellants—including naphtha, liquid oxygen, liquid hydrogen et cetera (taking into account the certainty that this ship would already have consumed a proportion of its fuel during initial acceleration)—and in no way can I account for the force of the blast described unless some entirely new principle of Science were employed. *Unless*— may I hazard?—Mass be regarded as a 'bound state' of Energy, only a tiny fraction of which Energy is released during the normal process of combustion. Were Mass to be totally convertible into Energy (by some method which I cannot yet envisage), then sufficient force might well be available to cause the destruction described.

This supposition set me to wondering about the sum total of heat which our planet receives yearly from the Sun—in view of the distance, size and probable age of that body. Were the Sun an ordinary 'bonfire' of gas, Sir, it would have consumed its whole substance long ago . . . !

This was followed by an appendix of mathematical calculations of which Anton could make neither head nor tail. He read the whole letter through again slowly from the beginning.

54

Perhaps he was still in a state of mental confusion due to the journey back from Kansk; and hence suggestible. Or maybe this letter from out of the blue did indeed address the question of how one could pay one's dues to Science in a manner more worthwhile than merely prospecting for meteoric ore ... Whatever the reason, the letter had an effect upon him equivalent to only one other piece of correspondence he had ever received in his life: four years before from D.V. Grigorovich hailing Anton as a new star in the literary firmament and exhorting him not to squander his talents as a hack.

However, this letter he now held in his hands wasn't from a Grand Old Man of the past addressing a young and careless tyro who might yet make good. It was from a man of the future, who had not yet had a chance to prove himself ...

Pouring the second instalment of his nightcap, Anton re-read the letter. Then he began scribbling calculations of his own, though these had nothing at all to do with ballistics or the energy value of naphtha.

He had already paid off a good half of his advance from Alexey Suvorin; and his books were still steadily netting cash for the *New Times* bookshop. Come the Spring, he'd been planning to ask Alexei Sergeyevich for another two or three thousand roubles advance, repayable over the next five years.

Why not right now?

Then there was this proposed fund which Suvorin mentioned ... Subscribers could well be lured by the prospect of meteoric wealth.

He must write post-haste, tomorrow, to Suvorin—and to this Konstantin Tsiolkovsky too.

Eventually Anton crawled into bed, his head spinning. Instantly he fell asleep, exhausted.

Ten

SO THEY SPENT their first night at the Artists' Retreat. Cloud had closed in hours earlier, hiding the mountains and the valley. Outside, snowflakes were swirling higgledy-piggledy in the light from the windows, though no great amount was actually settling. It was rather like being inside a child's snow-scene which was being tipped this way and that, constantly stirring up the same finite amount of white plastic flakes.

For supper, through in the dining room, Osip had dished up some hot beet soup with ham bones, followed by pickled sturgeon and boiled cabbage.

The dining room of the Retreat had been a minor ballroom once, before it had been crudely partitioned—leaving a blue plastered ceiling far too high for the space which remained, one moreover which curved upwards without ever curving down again. A single electric chandelier hung well off centre. The solitary window was huge, stretching from floor to ceiling, and draped in faded purple damask like a stage.

Conversation over supper was desultory; and this was not merely because Osip hung around to hear as much as he could.

Mikhail could be said to be in disgrace—were it not that Kirilenko was as fascinated as he was disconcerted by the strange turn that events had taken. While Kirilenko also would have been in disgrace—were the Doctor's expertise not the only straw left to cling to, as the film project foundered further into a chaos of unhistory . . .

Meanwhile Sonya Suslova was brooding. She was worried about her mentor's reputation, but still eagerly certain of his per-

56

spicacity. Thus she had begun to search out psychological motives by which to explain Mikhail's aberrant response to hypnosis. But this was not easy, since Mikhail was increasingly able to 'turn on' Anton at will and seemed blithely assured of the validity of his Anton; which made him a difficult case to analyse—for who was one analysing?

What's more, Sonya was starting to feel strongly attracted to this handsome chap—whichever chap he might be!—as so many ladies, years earlier, had felt drawn to Mr Chekhov. This sentiment was only intensified for her by the feeling of sensory deprivation in the Retreat, with the world beyond the walls blanked out.

Probably, Sonya decided, she was experiencing something akin to the imprinting of a newly-hatched duckling—upon its mother duck, or an old boot, whichever came first.

Yet she felt sure that she could help Mikhail therapeutically by a more direct form of involvement with him. In the sheets is truth, after all! Where was the harm in a bold initiative?

She knew perfectly well where the harm was, professionally. But by now absurdity seemed to have invaded all their lives, and it was certainly undermining hers. She felt detached from the realities of the present. It was as though she, Sonya, had been hypnotised—not Mikhail. Or as if the tobacco smoke curling upward from Kirilenko's briar pipe contained narcotics . . .

Anyway, Mikhail was making eyes at her, wasn't he? He seemed bent on enjoying every moment of the limelight—as much as he savoured the pickled sturgeon.

She puzzled. Anton had never been a ladies' man, had he? Perhaps Mikhail was only teasing her, in keeping with his other role . . .

Perhaps she ought to have a few words in private with Dr Kirilenko, about this confusion she was feeling? But he was too obviously preoccupied.

That night Sonya managed to control herself. She refrained from tiptoeing along the corridor at midnight.

However, when she awoke next morning, it was with a feeling of angry frustration, a sense of resentment that she had tossed an opportunity away. An opportunity to make a prime fool of herself? But she hardly cared about that. All the minor frustrations of her life seemed all at once to have reached a climax.

'That's more than can be said for me!' she thought bitterly.

She came downstairs to a breakfast of black bread, cherry jam and slices of Dutch-style cheese, to find Felix and Sergey already snapping away at each other across the table. As nobody else was in the room yet, Sonya went over to the window to avoid getting involved.

Not one single external object was visible. Not a tree, not a bush, not a stone. A blank white covering of snow hid what she remembered to be a paved path running right around the building; the thin even layer was as neat as a newly tucked-in sheet. As for the rest of the world, well, the Retreat might as well have been floating in mid-air in the heart of a cumulus cloud. There was only a dense white mist, woolly and indefinite, unmoving.

"What weather!" she exclaimed . . .

. . . just as Dr Kirilenko swept into the dining room, arm in arm with Mikhail, an elder statesman leading his protégé.

"I've been giving a lot of thought to our little difficulty," he said without preamble. "Now, it's possible to project a hypnotic subject into a *future* role, as well as a past one. And when I say 'future', naturally I'm referring to the future as foreseen on the basis of subconsciously available data. The popular journalists might be tempted to describe this as 'Reincarnation in the Future'—"

Sergey glared malevolently.

"—though needless to say it has no connexion with an afterlife in some future body—no more than yesterday's work had anything to do with actual reincarnation! And when I say 'actual', I must remind you that no such thing as reincarnation exists, except in popular fancy. *Nevertheless*, an element of genuine precognition may well be present in such exercises. If it could be properly developed a superability of this type would make the work of Futurology less of a guessing game."

"*Sod* your Futurology," said Sergey. "I've got a script to get together. Preferably this weekend."

When Kirilenko first came in, Sonya had quickly sat at table and helped herself to a slice of cheese. Now she found in her agitation that she was spreading the cheese with jam . . .

"I think what Gorodsky *means*," said Felix heavily, "is that while you would win our riveted attention at any other time, right now we have a more pressing problem on our plate."

"Quite!" Kirilenko refused to take offence. "So what I propose for our first session today is to tell Mike that he has already successfully *completed* his role in *Chekhov's Journey*. In his mind, he will be living in the future. The film will already be . . . in the can. This may, ah, clear the stage . . ."

Without further ado, as though it wasn't up to Felix to yea or nay this suggestion, Kirilenko proceeded to sit down and tuck into cherry jam from the orchards down Irkutsk way.

"Any port in a storm," muttered Sergey direly. "To quote our beloved Fedotik."

Sonya discovered that jam spread on cheese was really quite tasty. This was just as well, since she could hardly scrape it off again, in front of them all.

Mikhail grinned at her. "Onward to the future!"

Eleven

COMMANDER ANTON ASTROV was astonished to see a fly drifting midway in the observation pod of the *K.E. Tsiolkovsky*. He rubbed his eyes in disbelief, but the fly was still there. It buzzed impotently, and turned round and round in circles. How in the name of all that was wonderful had a fly got on board the ship? It eclipsed a star as he watched.

A common house fly! Not a bluebottle or a horsefly or anything exotic like a tsetse fly . . . Just a common house fly. It was astonishing enough in itself.

Really, he ought to catch it sharpish and snuff it out. Yet sentiment overwhelmed him. That wretched little fly was a tiny living portion of the earthly biosphere—and it was about to leave solar space for ever and for ever. As such, it seemed uniquely precious.

'I've got myself a pet at last!' he thought in amazement. 'A pet fly, of all things!'

Bringing out a little plastic box of space-sickness gum, he emptied the contents carefully back into his zippered pocket and secured them. A gentle push, and a few seconds later he caught the fly in the box with all the neatness of a deep orbit station receiving the docking of a supply craft. He shut the lid. The insect could gain some purchase now. The box zizz-zizzed in his fingers as the fly flopped and somersaulted, wings vibrating feverishly.

"Little pet," he addressed the box, "I name thee Pandora." He tucked it into a smaller zippered pocket. "Mustn't forget that it's you in there! Butterflies in the tummy are one thing—but a fly? That's another matter . . ."

A moment later his continuing trajectory carried him up against the thick radiation-proof plasticrystal—stronger than steel—which formed the transparent hull of the pod. Gripping the nearest hand-hold, he hung just a few centimetres away from hard vacuum and gazed at the three-quarters-lit Earth. It was a fine day over the Indian Ocean and much of Asia. What little he could see of the Soviet Union was up near the visual North Pole.

'They'll think I'm nuts, talking to a fly when we're about to set off for the stars! But it's this sort of thing that makes a man, a man . . .

'And a woman, a woman,' he reflected. For his Astrogator, Sasha Sorina, had just poked her flaxen curls up through the hatch from the Control Room. Her blue eyes regarded him coolly: those same eyes which would soon pick out a suitable star with a habitable world orbiting it a couple of hundred or couple of thousand light years towards the antapex of the Sun's motion— Right Ascension 90°, Declination 34° South—far beyond the stars composing the visible constellation of Columba . . .

How far, of course, depended on how many times they would have to jump through the Flux before they found themselves close enough to a suitable new sun.

"We're nearly ready, Commander. I thought I heard you calling."

"No, no. I was just wondering aloud whether they'll ever build a second Flux-ship . . ." The less said to her about pet flies, the better.

" 'They'?"

"I mean, us. The Soviet Union. It's so altruistic, isn't it? Sending out a colony when you can never receive any news of it."

Sasha was beautiful, but she was very literal-minded. "But wouldn't there be a paradox of cause and effect, if they *could* hear from us? We jump one hundred years back through time, and this puts us a hundred light years downstream of the Sun's motion round the Galaxy. Anything less, and a radio message could reach the Earth before we even set off!"

"What bothers me," remarked Anton flippantly, "is what exactly happens if we don't find a suitable star? Shall we just keep on jumping back along the Earth's world-line? If we go far enough we'll circle the Galaxy, and catch up with Earth a couple of hundred thousand years ago—and we'll colonise it in desperation!"

"And become our own ancestors?" Sasha looked affronted.

'And my pet fly, the ancestor of a mighty dynasty of flies . . .'

"The Universe doesn't allow such things. The Principle of Cosmic Censorship absolutely forbids subversion of cause and effect. We'll find our star, never fear! Humanity will colonise the cosmos."

"A little bit of the cosmos, anyway . . . Hmm, it's a pity the Flux-Field has a one-track mind. If we could go anywhere we pleased—"

"But the Principle of World-Line Constancy strongly dictates—"

"Sure it does. Just wishing, that's all."

"It's a far nobler use *we're* putting the Flux to, than those mad Americans."

Captain America's Shield: she was right, there . . .

The official reason for the Flux-Shield, which could be switched on at a moment's notice to blanket America, was that if any giant meteor or comet-head came zooming in on collision course with US territory, the Shield would bat it on its way—zipping it ten years into the past and ten light years in the direction of Columba, a piece of symbolism which no doubt appealed to those in power in District Columbia . . .

But likewise with any Soviet satellite or missile platform overflying US territory. With a flick of the wrist these, too, could be knocked right out of the stadium. Any war, now, would simply leave Earth's path through space ten billion billion kilometres hindwards littered with missiles and satellites and Soviet personnel staring glumly out at the interstellar void—like a trail of beer cans bobbing far to the rear of the liner, Earth.

Sasha drifted to Anton's side; together they peered along the ship. All supply ferries had departed some hours ago, leaving the *K. E. Tsiolkovsky* alone in deep orbit a safe distance beyond the reach of Captain America's Shield—should any malicious soul in Cheyenne feel tempted to send them on their way, untimely. Why should anyone do so? Why, out of sheer irritation. Since there was no reason at all why a starship should be streamlined, their ship was built in the shape of a huge Hammer and Sickle.

The hammer shaft contained the fusion reactor jets capable of carrying them up to half a light year, once Sasha decided they were close enough to a friendly star system. The sickle shaft contained storage bays, and the polished blade of the sickle itself was a huge sweep of solar power cells. At the geometrical centre of the ship, where both shafts intersected, was the Flux-Drive. And up here in the head of the hammer were the crew quarters and control section; directly beneath this a thousand hypnotised colonists lay in yogic trance in rack upon rack, their body functions ticking over at a hundredth of the normal metabolic rate.

How very provoking to the Americans to see the Hammer and Sickle thus floating in space! But in another hour or so it would disappear forever, to become the little moon of another world. The onboard shuttles would descend ten times over, till the moon was empty. Thereafter the celestial Hammer and Sickle would shine down forever more upon New Earth as an orbiting monument, the only possible link—a symbolic one—with the USSR.

Being alone with Sasha Sorina, with only the stars staring in, Anton Astrov thought of kissing her impetuously to celebrate. But she might slap him for impertinence. It wouldn't do to start the greatest voyage of all time with a red handprint on one's cheek.

Twelve

ON THE MORNING when Countess Zelenina called on Anton at the Staraya Rossiya Hotel on Blagoryeshtchenskaya, he was suffering a recurrence of one of his old enemies: migraine.

It was only a mild attack as yet, compared with previous bouts, but he took it as a warning sign. Was it possible that all his old familiar foes—which he thought he had abandoned on the Siberian plain, somewhere between Omsk and Tomsk—were even now hastening to catch up with him? Were his haemorrhoids rolling along the Road within striking distance of Krasnoyarsk? Was his gastritis likewise oozing this way? All because he had dallied in one place too long?

At the bedroom door Anton begged to excuse himself, but the Countess practically forced her way into the room. He yielded, and called to a passing maid to order tea.

Lydia Zelenina was a tall slim woman with a fine oval face. Her hair was chestnut, and her eyes dark and bold, their lashes thickly 'seductive'. At thirty-two she was a widow, whose husband—a rich local merchant—had perished from cholera three summers earlier, leaving her with two young daughters and a large town house, as well as income from forestry, lumber mills and tanneries. Unfortunately she tended to smoke and drink; this marred her somewhat in Anton's eyes.

Today she was attired eccentrically—in riding boots, a black brocaded gown, and (considering that it was the height of summer) an impossibly hot fur hat the size of a rook's nest. She looked as though she had set out for a ball, to be held immediately after a funeral, but suspected she might have to escape from a wolf pack *en route*.

Her noble grandfather had been exiled to Krasnoyarsk back in '25 for taking part in the Decembrist plot. Accompanied by his loyal wife, together they had become part of the kernel of civilizing forces which eventually made this town a decent place to live in. Lydia inherited a penchant for conspiring, in the shape of organising social events, and for wild deeds . . .

When tea arrived, she lit a cigarette. Mostly she held it far from her lips, puffing only a couple of defiant billows into the air. After a while she crossed her legs with a flourish, to display to best effect her smartly tooled boots which were so much more finely cut than Anton's own tormentors.

He regarded her through his pince-nez in silence. At last she crushed out her cigarette amidst the stubs of Anton's own roll-ups.

"*Mon cher* Anton Pavlovich, I'm sure there are secrets hidden in your silence—secrets which no one will ever know!"

"If that's so, Countess, they must be a secret from me too . . ." Actually, he had been thinking about gastritis.

She disregarded his wry smile. "No, I mean it: just as surely as there's a secret locked in the silent heart of the taiga! *En tout cas*, that's why I'm here. *Voyez*: we aren't all illiterates in Siberia. I propose that we should raise funds for your coming expedition by means of a benefit performance of your delicious farce, *The Bear*."

Anton could have groaned aloud. That stupid piece of vaudeville, hacked out for provincial clowns to laugh their silly heads off at!

On the other hand, he *had* been living off the proceeds of its wretched nonsense for the best part of last year . . .

"I would be delighted to take the role of the widow Popova, myself."

Oh yes. Undoubtedly. *Ça va sans dire*. And which of her suitors would she nominate for the part of the 'Bear', Smirnov? With whom did she wish to conduct a flaming row in public? And challenge to a duel? And wave a revolver at? Ah yes: with her eyes

65

sparkling and her face a-flush—gunpowder and fireworks pop-ping off at every word! And which of her rivals, amongst the ticket holders in the audience, would she glare at whilst issuing her challenge? Had Countess Zelenina perhaps found a packet of her *own* former husband's *billets-doux* locked up in some drawer after his death, exactly as Popova had?

"I think we shall stage it at the Governor's residence. He was a good friend of Zelenin's . . . *Mais écoutez*, there's more: I'm quite a rich woman—I'm sure I may speak frankly!—and I would be more than happy to pay a substantial donation towards the cost of mounting the Tunguska Expedition, provided that—"

"Provided what?"

"Provided that I go along."

"*Eh?*"

"I want to accompany the expedition. I shan't hold you back. I don't expect any comfort. I anticipate danger and privation. Oh Anton Pavlovich, I'm so sick of frittering my life away on petty excitements. Dances or a duck shoot—what nonsense!"

"I hardly think you fully understand—"

"Women regularly go through childbirth, *mon ami*. I don't think you know how much toughness and courage it requires of us!"

'No,' thought Anton, 'and you haven't seen what it's like when it goes wrong . . .'

"I doubt if a man could endure it!"

"Fortunately, we don't often have to, Countess . . . But it wasn't your stamina I was questioning. If I might be blunt: one woman, alone in the wilderness with a band of men?"

"Oh, you're worried about my reputation?" She fluttered her eyelashes. "Or are you worried about *yours?*"

'Good God,' he thought, 'she's making a pitch at me. Be careful, Antosha, old son! On the other hand, don't rebuff her—that's dodgy, too. A woman spurned, and all that!'

He spoke jocularly. "I've heard tell there are giant *rats* out in the taiga."

"You know perfectly well that's just a tall story. And quite unworthy of *Doctor* Chekhov, the explorer of Tunguska! I'm completely serious."

'Yes, you are. That's the trouble . . .'

"I do hope, Countess, that you won't challenge me to a duel if I greet your proposal with a certain degree of—"

"*Ecoutez*: I can shoot straight. I can ride."

"What, on pack horses? We'll be walking most of the time."

"I'd *advise* you to take a sledge or two."

"That's assuming we ever do set off . . ."

"You will, with my assistance." Lighting another cigarette, she waved it around as though the whole matter was signed, sealed and delivered.

"If you'll permit me to say so, Countess, you aren't qualified scientifically. To make observations, for example . . ."

"Oh, as to that, I happen to own a camera—and you won't find its like anywhere east of the Urals. It's the latest type, imported from Germany. No more fussing on with heavy glass plates—this one uses roll-film."

"What's that? What's roll-film?" he asked, unguardedly.

Lydia smiled in triumph. "See? You do need a photographic expert. You hadn't even thought of that! What's more, I don't see why you need go on spending money in this dreadful hotel. *Quel ennui*! It must be so confining. I should count myself privileged if you were to accept the hospitality of my own home." She wagged a finger at him. "With *no* obligations to be on show to casual visitors—or pay any attention whatsoever to my darling daughters. You wouldn't be bothered at all. You needn't even be present at rehearsals of *The Bear*. Though, if you like, I *could* initiate you into the mysteries of a roll-film camera." She winked. "Click!"—as though snapping his photograph.

Anton shifted about uncomfortably in his seat, and as he did so he felt a brief pang in his bum.

He had to admit it: he'd been stuck in this hotel far too long. Writing letters to all and sundry. Squeezing out articles about the taiga and the Tunguska Mystery. The room wasn't exactly luxurious . . .

Lydia leapt up and clapped her hands, knocking ash on to the threadbare carpet. "I take it that's settled! What are you waiting for? Get your bags packed, *mon ami*."

Thirteen

"THE WHOLE POINT of the film is Chekhov's bloody journey!" swore Sergey in a passion. "*Not* how he sits on his ass in bloody Krasnoyarsk scribbling about something that happened eighteen years later when he was bloody dead!"

Mikhail sprang to the defence of his alter ego. "I'm still planning a pretty heroic journey, ain't I? It's just in a different direction, that's all."

And Sonya thought: 'How like a Caribbean pirate Mikhail looks, with that patch over his eye! Like Captain Blood . . . Or—like Commander Astrov, with a pet fly perched on his shoulder instead of a parrot.' She giggled quietly. Sergey directed a withering glare at her.

Outside, blank white mist continued to hide everything: a thick milky haze, a host of particles suspended in an ocean . . . an ocean of time . . .

"Commander Anton Astrov . . ." Sonya only realized that she had uttered the words aloud, when it was too late to recall them.

"Ah. Yes, indeed. Hmm. The Astrov business . . ." Kirilenko was visibly embarrassed. "One point I ought to have emphasized earlier on is that it's quite *difficult* to—how shall we put it?—articulate the future, except in a caricature-like manner. By that, I mean this . . ." Kirilenko chuckled with false heartiness. "Ah, what a grammatical solecism I have just perpetrated! Still, if we Russians must possess such a subtle language that we don't even know the declensions of all our nouns . . . ! But never mind. Let me put this question to you: What would a man of the eighteenth century make of a television set? He would have to assume that it was an ingenious camera obscura. And what would he make of the mushroom cloud from an atom bomb? Why, probably it would look like a volcanic eruption."

"What's your point, man?" said Felix. "Is there one? Or are you just babbling?"

"I never babble, Felix Moseivich. My point is that Mikhail must necessarily misinterpret the future—in terms of today. He symbolises, in other words. Hence the Hammer and Sickle starship, and the cartoon book name of the American defence system."

Sonya spoke impetuously. "But *is* there a starship of some sort? A ship that travels backwards through time and space?" She carried on pell-mell, ignoring Kirilenko's look of reproof. "What I mean is: why this *particular* thing? Why this kind of starship rather than something else? He says that the American war-shield works on the same basic principle, doesn't he? So why shouldn't this represent a genuine precognition? A glimpse of a technique which will actually exist one day?"

Kirilenko drummed his fingers rapidly on the arm of his chair, and when he answered it was in a quick, quiet, tight voice.

"If he's picking up authentic information, it's possible that he's milking the brains of some researcher in the present—not the future. From somewhere nearby. Maybe the Krasnoyarsk Institute of Physics—they do space research there. Or maybe further afield, somewhere secret . . . This might put us all in a highly embarrassing, not to say dangerous position." Kirilenko tapped his nose meaningfully. "The less said about this possibility, the better. Thankfully it has no relevance at all to Anton Chekhov—or to the Tunguska fireworks."

"I thought," said Sergey, "you were trying to get him to forecast the outcome of the bloody film? Or have we all forgotten that the film has nothing whatever to do with bloody Tunguska?"

"He does seem to have gone a bit astray," allowed Kirilenko.

Sergey guffawed. "At least he's consistent! Astray in the past, astray in the future."

"You must agree it's a fascinating case."

"So that's what you call it?"

"Well, don't blame *me*!" said Mikhail. "I was doing my darnedest to focus on *Chekhov's Journey*. Honest! But my own personal film speeded up incredibly—and suddenly I was Anton Astrov instead. Chatting up my luscious, prosaic Astrogator."

"What exactly do you mean by your 'own personal' film?" Felix asked him.

"It's hard to express. As far as I'm concerned, this hypnosis business feels just like watching a film—but acting in it at the same time, if you get me. I'm watching myself act, but from inside . . ."

"Nobody blames you," Sonya assured him. How could Mike possibly regard her as prosaic? If he could only know the hot flushes of confusion which had assaulted her the night before . . . and which she had nobly overcome.

'Hot flushes, indeed!' She rebuked herself. 'I'm behaving like a fatuous provincial wife, straight out of Chekhov, about to ruin herself in some idiotic love affair!'

There was a cursory knock at the double door, and immediately Osip stepped uninvited into the room.

"What do you want?" demanded Felix.

"Just thought you comrades might like to know our phone's packed up . . . Must be the snow, eh?"

"And who the devil were you phoning?"

Osip looked blank. "Eh? Just picked the phone up to dust it."

Fourteen

AS SOON AS he was installed in the Zelenin residence, Anton's health promptly picked up. No more migraine, no more itchings in the arse.

The daughters Nastya and Masha were as chalk and cheese to each other. Nastya, the elder, was small and serious. She was a self-possessed witness of everything which went on—a sort of house spy. While her younger sister Masha was taller by a head, willowy, erratic and highly-strung.

Presiding over these ill-matched girls were a young German governess, Olga Franzovna, who was addicted to card tricks, and Polena the fat old nursemaid, skivvy and cook. Definitely this was a woman's household—even if the Countess and the governess were both wayward types—so Anton soon settled down into a tolerably familiar mould. He wrote to Moscow. He wrote to Borovsk. He prepared lists and tore them up. He visited local suppliers together with Jaroslav Mirek, haggled and drew up more lists. Some money began arriving from Moscow and Petersburg.

Meanwhile, daily in the drawing room, rehearsals of *The Bear* took place—far more rehearsals than such a brief one-act skit could possibly require. However, the Countess was true to her promise, and Anton was not asked to involve himself in these—though he soon grew heartily sick of the sound of his own trivial lines resounding from the drawing room. The three actors seemed to have become absurdly addicted to the little play. They rehearsed it over and over with such fervent dedication that it might have been a religious Mass he had written.

Playing opposite Lydia in the role of Popova was . . . Baron

Nikolai Vershinin, ideally cast as the bear with the sore head. Dr Rodé took the part of the old servant Looka; and Vasily Fedotik always accompanied his two friends to act, nominally, as prompter. Since the actors soon knew their lines backwards, Fedotik was quite *de trop* in this capacity—which was a considerable relief to him. Too much attention to the printed word was bad for the eyesight. So while the principals shouted and rumbled to each other, he whiled away his time happily at a card table, playing patience with himself. Occasionally Olga Franzovna joined him, to show off her repertoire of card tricks.

After a week or so Anton realized that there was more to these endless rehearsals than met the eye . . .

For Lydia was indeed a dashing widow, even more liable to discharge a duelling pistol in real life than she was in art. And Vershinin was indeed an abusive, bellowing fellow—with a soft heart underneath. What was actually happening in that drawing room, under the pretext of rehearsals, was a kind of courtship ritual.

How many more times would these two embrace each other passionately, to the astonishment of Looka-Rodé . . . before they embraced in reality?

Once Anton understood this, his discomfort at hearing the silly lines so oft repeated began to fade away—together with his earlier suspicion that the Countess might make an amatory bee-line for *him* . . .

From Olga Kundasova a package of books arrived, and Anton began to learn all about meteors, comets, asteroids and planet-oids—without ever experiencing a single twinge from haem-orrhoids.

So the summer wore hotly on. Until one day when—funded by Suvorin, who had also pulled strings at Anton's request—there arrived in Krasnoyarsk on several months' leave of absence from his elementary school: Konstantin Tsiolkovsky himself.

And at once Anton wondered whether he had made a serious error of judgement . . .

Tsiolkovsky arrived on the Zelenin doorstep late one afternoon. Polena opened the door for him, and shrieked in alarm, bringing Lydia and Olga and Anton hastening to her aid. For it seemed a moot point whether the emaciated tramp who stood there ought not to proceed onwards to the nearest hospital ward.

Granted that Tsiolkovsky was worn out by a long and tiresome journey—and nobody could reasonably expect a traveller who had just traversed the Siberian plain to arrive with his clothing anything other than soiled, crumpled and decorated with straw. Yet Tsiolkovsky appeared to have neglected to eat a scrap during the entire journey. His eyes peered out weakly through cheap spectacles. What's more, it immediately became clear—in spite of the size of the man's ears with their long dangling lobes—that he was almost deaf; certainly he seemed to have dire difficulty in communicating. This picture of misery was completed by a cheap suitcase tied together with string. In short Tsiolkovsky looked just like the most wretched type of deported exile.

Nevertheless, once the man had succeeded in identifying himself, Lydia Zelenina drew him graciously inside—though she raised an eyebrow.

"Most honoured Sir!" Dropping his suitcase, Tsiolkovsky blundered into Anton's embrace, and the two men hugged each other—rather more dutifully than devotedly on Anton's part.

"Polena, we will eat dinner much earlier than usual."

The old woman nodded to her mistress, and bustled off, casting back glances of pity and contempt. What was this fellow, then: a house guest or a refugee?

Right there in the hall, Tsiolkovsky knelt down and began to unpick the string from his suitcase, as if he expected that he would have to doss down before the front door like a watchdog. Meanwhile the two young sisters had crept up behind a pillar to peer at him: Masha wide-eyed and giggling, Nastya with the narrowed gaze of a police agent.

From amidst a jumble of dirty crushed laundry Tsiolkovsky

produced a manuscript bound with a frayed blue ribbon. This he presented to Anton.

"Thought perhaps . . . thought maybe . . . after dinner? As an entertainment?" Tsiolkovsky choked. "Better at expressing myself on paper!" Did Anton's ears deceive him or did Tsiolkovsky speak Russian with a faint trace of a Polish accent?

The manuscript was entitled *On the Moon*, and was penned in a neat, sloping copperplate hand.

Oh well, this had to be that same piece of—what had he called it in his first letter, Science Fantasy? A glance confirmed that the pages were a first-person narrative. Undoubtedly the very same. I hold, thought Anton, an infant *genre* in my hands. He was careful not to drop it.

"Olga," said the Countess loudly, "would you kindly show this gentleman up to his room?"

Tsiolkovsky gaped. "Room? Eh? Oh yes—"

Rather better groomed and with his beard combed out, Konstantin Tsiolkovsky sat down at table a couple of hours later. The instruction to Polena to hurry might as well have been spoken in Chinese. But no doubt she had the welfare of the other dinner guests equally in mind. This evening, these were Mirek, and Ilya Sidorov.

The meal commenced with kidney and cucumber soup accompanied by several glasses of vodka which presently loosened Tsiolkovsky's tongue, though they did little to improve his powers of hearing. While Olga and Lydia quizzed Tsiolkovsky about the hazards of his journey, Anton tried to assess the man.

He had already glanced through *On the Moon*, and a peculiar piece of fiction it was indeed—all about lunar latitude and longitude, and thermal conductivity and light intensity, and the joys of feeling the chains of gravity slacken; wrapped up in the form of a dream. Pleasantly enough written, on the whole, but hopelessly didactic!

Watching the man slurp down three helpings of Polena's soup

75

while trying to conduct a conversation, Anton couldn't but recognize an element of wish-fulfilment in the tale. Could its author only but cut the dash that his characters did—striding the landscape in great leaping bounds! Of course, Anton could sympathize with such a fantasy, having only recently hauled his own prematurely ageing carcase half way across Siberia, full of envy for the birds. But really, there was no irony in this Konstantin Eduardovich.

Soup was followed by roast duck and stewed cabbage.

"Let us imagine," said Tsiolkovsky between mouthfuls, "a cosmic spaceship . . . powered by the same principle as the sun itself . . . ! When it came to its doom it was as though a miniature sun had exploded . . . using up an aeon's energy in an instant."

Sidorov spoke slowly and loudly, as to the deaf. "Do you mean to say this spaceship was powered by jets of gas?"

"No, no! The sun cannot burn its fuel . . . in the way a gas-jet burns. Somehow the very *atoms* of the sun . . . must burst apart."

"An atom's indivisible," Mirek said. "Everybody knows that. "It's the smallest piece of matter you can have."

Tsiolkovsky cupped a hand behind his ear; Mirek repeated the objection.

"Aha, but what if it isn't the smallest? What if it only seems to be so . . . because each atom is locked together with immense force? Once we can survey the true extent of the destruction, I can calculate the energy needed—it'll be possible to estimate the strength of this 'binding force' . . . What's more, how will these broken bits of atoms behave? Maybe they'll fly around frantically . . . trying to join up again? Maybe they'll run smack into other atoms . . . and split them too?"

"If broken atoms hit a living body," said Sidorov, excitedly, "I mean, if they burrow into living cells . . . I'm thinking about those scabs on the reindeer!"

"Exactly. But medicine isn't my province." Tsiolkovsky nodded deferentially at Anton, and crammed more cabbage into his mouth.

76

Anton smiled. "I assure you, I know nothing whatever about Broken-Atom Sickness . . ."

"Equally . . . if we were to bombard chosen inorganic substances . . . in a controlled way, with broken atoms—perhaps we could deliberately transform one element into another? A bar of lead . . . into a bar of gold."

"That isn't science," protested Mirek. "That's alchemy. Look, the atom is called an atom—from the Greek—because you can't divide it. We might find a lot of iron and nickel and tin buried under the taiga, but I can guarantee we aren't going to find gold."

"Eh?"

"I said—"

"I heard what you said, Mr Mirek. I didn't say there was any gold—aren't you listening? What I said was, we might find evidence of a spaceship from another world, powered by a form of propulsion . . . undreamed of at present. With respect, I'm afraid your attitude's all too typical. Too many scientists are bound by mental chains."

"Quite!" Sidorov nodded sagely. "All your conventional professors—I've said it before: Lord Nelson's blind eye!"

"I myself have the dubious privilege of being self-educated . . ." Tsiolkovsky tried to scrape some more duck flesh from a bare bone. "I taught myself in isolation from professors, laboratories and universities . . . Of course this can lead to ignorance of the latest scientific progress, but I also believe it yields a freshness of approach . . . a willingness to look at phenomena from a new viewpoint—*provided*, always, that the mathematics is correct! My dear Sir, just because science tells us that an atom can't be divided and uses a Greek word to say so, doesn't make it a fact for ever more."

"Bravo!" applauded Sidorov.

"We need to keep our minds open, gentlemen. And ladies. If the evidence discredits my hypothesis of a spaceship, I'll be the first one to discard it. With regret, true . . . Yet without defending it blindly to the death, as is so often the case."

"If we *do* find broken bits of a spaceship from another world," began Lydia.

"No, no!" Tsiolkovsky interrupted her. "There won't be any broken bits."

"I thought you said—"

"I said broken atoms—that's different. This isn't like an artillery shell exploding, showering pieces of metal around. The ship would be totally evaporated."

This touched Lydia's heart. "Alas, what sort of brave creatures can have been in it?"

Perhaps because her voice was higher in pitch, Tsiolkovsky heard her perfectly. "Creatures possessed of noble intentions, I promise you! Only the nobly-minded will heed the call of the cosmos."

As the conversation proceeded, and as duck was succeeded by stewed gooseberries with cream, Anton decided with relief that he hadn't made such an error of judgement after all. Vagabond though he looked, and blunt though his manners were at times, this Tsiolkovsky was a man of vision and endurance and honest rationality. Perhaps it was unfair to expect him to have insight into the human heart as well . . .

They repaired to the drawing room after dinner. With Lydia's nodded consent, Mirek commandeered a bottle of vodka *en route*. Olga Franzovna seated herself promptly at the piano and proceeded to butcher a transcription of the first movement of Peter Tchaikovsky's *Fifth Symphony*. In despair at her heavy-handedness—compared with her legerdemain at cards—Anton fled upstairs to fetch Tsiolkovsky's manuscript.

Returning, he passed this over to its author before the governess could commence murdering the second movement; fortunately Olga took the hint, and retired from the piano.

"Konstantin Eduardovich would like to entertain us with a short shory he's written—with your permission, Countess?"

"With your stamp of approval on it, Anton Pavlovich, how could anyone possibly refuse . . . ?"

Tsiolkovsky adopted a pedagogic stance in front of the fireplace. In the stilted style of a teacher dictating out of a Chemistry textbook, he at once began to read his tale of science fantasy. Fortunately, once the narrative moved on to the heady delights of flying through the air under one's own steam, freed from the oppressive pull of Earth, his delivery improved markedly. His voice thrilled; he seemed intoxicated, like a religious ecstatic. Sidorov watched him devotedly all the while, wearing the expression of a loyal hound whose master has just returned home after a six months absence . . .

Afterwards, and it was quite a long while afterwards, everyone applauded the unusual story. Olga Franzovna jumped up and pirouetted around. Casting discretion to the winds, Lydia joined her, and together the two women whirled around the room like a swiftly rotating planet and its attendant moon.

Fifteen

"TIME FOR ONE last tour of inspection, Sorina!"

If a common house fly could have sneaked into the observation pod, what else might be lying around which oughtn't to be?

"But we're almost ready, Commander."

"Damn it, I want to look round the ship! You'll accompany me, Sorina—that's an order."

Together they floated upside-down into the control room, where Second Officer Yuri Valentin was fiddling with the Fluxtime gauges. He seemed to be having a spot of bother with the chronodyne resonometer.

"Well, *he* ain't ready."

Valentin grinned. "Slight imbalance, that's all. Fix it in a jiffy."

Chief Engineer Anna Aksakova was busy checking the fusion-drive master switches. Screens glowed with schematics; tell-tales winked on and off. And all around Sasha Sorina's vacated bay video screens were showing sections of starfield, and the Earth, Moon and Sun (with glare compensation). Her Deep Space Radar was up and running, tracking satellites and debris . . .

"You've no imagination, that's the trouble," Anton said to Sasha. "What was it that Mayakovsky said about the bureaucrats holding back time?"

"I'm sure I don't know."

He drifted to the open hatch giving access to the upper transverse corridor. "'*Time Forward*!' That's what his Five Year Plan proclaimed. And soon a great big time machine was invented. But all the bureaucrats got shaken out of it, and left behind . . ."

"Really!" she protested, indignant.

80

"Or how about Zamyatin? 'In the name of Tomorrow, we judge Today!' How about that for a rallying cry?" Bracing himself in the hatch, he launched off in the direction of the Phys and Chem labs. The fat steel tube of the corridor was painted a restful sky blue, and lit with fluorescent strips. Spaced evenly a metre apart on each side, hand grips were set like rungs so that personnel wouldn't collide with one another.

"But," came her rational tones from behind, "we'll be going back through time—not forwards."

"Aha! Do you fear we'll be forced to recapitulate history? Do you imagine we'll need to live through another feudal age and another capitalist era before we reach utopia?"

"I didn't say anything of the sort! Imagining such things is the job of our Social Planning Officer."

"Imagination is a job? How neatly you prove Mayakovsky's point."

Anton caught hold of the final rung, at the intersection corridor before the Chem Lab.

"I mean, he'll see to it that we don't become feudal or bourgeois."

"Oh, old Saratov'll give it a try. He'll have the Hammer and Sickle up in orbit to point at, won't he?"

A vertical shaft descended through the decks nearby: one of the free fall 'elevators'. Out of it popped a shuttle pilot, in her yellow serge zipper-suit. Gripping a rung, she saluted.

"Never mind the formalities. Hurry up!" Anton turned to Sasha, now clinging close behind him. "You see? I didn't find a mouse gumming up the works—but I found a shuttle pilot out of station." The pilot was already floating swiftly towards Phys. "Oh, and talking of the old Hammer and Sickle up in the sky, wouldn't it be a laugh if we kind of *regressed*—and ended up worshipping it, as a sign of power in the heavens? Praying to it for rain!"

"How you ever passed screening for this command, I'll never know," said Sasha in amazement.

81

"Maybe it takes a merry nutter to command a ship like this?" Anton patted the little box in his pocket. "My apologies, Sorina! I'm a bit nervous—like the proverbial virgin on her wedding night, eh?"

She sniffed. "That happy event will occur some while *after* we establish our colony."

"You'd better watch out for Saratov, old girl. He might want all the women locked up in a breeding harem for the first ten generations."

"As though he would! You know perfectly well our colony can only function properly with *active* participations by all female personnel. As soon as I stop being Astrogator, I become a Land Surveyor."

"I didn't think you'd become a Comedienne." Anton pushed through into Chem, catching hold of the mass spectrometer to look round the lab for any flasks of acid poised to crash into the walls whenever acceleration surged. None were. Three chemists in cream and blue tunics were buckled in their seats.

"Good, good," he said vaguely. Feeling vindicated, he thrust back through the hatch, and deliberately bumped into Sonya. Gripping her momentarily, he whispered, "We must preserve the gene for humour. Other worlds, other jokes!"

When they arrived back in the control room, Yuri Valentin seemed to have satisfied himself that the resonometer was working properly in full harmony with all his other gauges: the temporal symptomometer, retardograph, horologe, horometer, isocalendar and datalscope.

"Drive and attitude jets primed for instant firing," reported Anna, while Anton and Sasha buckled themselves into their padded seats. Ideally, these jets shouldn't need to be fired instantly, but there was always a microscopic chance that the ship might emerge from the Flux on collision course with something: an asteroid, the photosphere of a sun, whatever.

"Okay, Yuri, blow the horn."

82

A klaxon hooted through the ship half a dozen times.

"P.A. system patched in to the Motherland?"

"Aye, aye. Now."

Anton flicked on his chin-mike. "This is Commander Astrov of the Flux-ship *K. E. Tsiolkovsky* calling Earth. Comrades, at your word we're ready to proceed—out into the unknown cosmos."

Crackle-crackle . . .

Ground Control in Siberia delivered a short, uplifting speech to which Anton presently replied in kind, wishing that he could lift up a glass of vodka to toast the mission. Who was the distillery specialist amongst the colonists? he wondered.

". . . You may proceed at your discretion!"

Actually, Ground Control had controlled nothing since the last supply ship left. Anton flipped off his mike for a moment.

"You know, folks, we've just become an independent state."

"An autonomous socialist republic," Sasha said sternly.

He reactivated his mike. "This is your Commander speaking. Secure yourselves! We go into the Flux in exactly five minutes from now. Our first time-jump will carry us one hundred and fifty-seven light years. This should bring us to within three light months of a target star which has already been verified from Earth by telescope as 'promising'. According to the scientists this jump should seem quasi-instantaneous, which I gather is their way of saying that it might seem to occupy several minutes. Once we emerge, remember that it'll take us several hours of work to confirm the presence of an Earth-type planet. And if there isn't one, off we'll jump again. Let's hope it's 'first time lucky'. Good luck to us all!" And off with the mike.

"Right, that's that bit over. Departure in four minutes, twenty seconds. Hit the button on my word, Anna."

Anton spent the remaining time softly whistling melodies from the *1812 Overture*. As it happened, when departure time arrived he was in the middle of the Czarist national anthem.

Sixteen

"GEE, I'M SORRY about all this," said Mikhail. "I can't seem to throw this Astrov guy. It's as though I'm glued to the seat of a swing. Back I go in one direction, and I bump into Anton Pavlovich and his Tunguska cronies. Off I go the other way, and Commander Astrov grabs hold of me. I feel like a pendulum."

Impenetrable fog still wrapped the Retreat. Nor had the phone service been restored. Sonya Suslova stood up and stretched.

"I feel like a walk—anybody coming?"

Mikhail also got to his feet.

"Don't go too far," cautioned Felix. "You could get lost out there. Once round the building, or just a little way down the road—do you hear?"

As the two of them were on the point of leaving the room, Kirilenko spoke up.

"It's curious, you know? What Mike's experiencing is like a 'wave function', stretching between past and future. In 1890 there's one amplitude peak. There's another one in Commander Astrov's time. And here's our observation point, in the present. Neither the Tunguska past nor the Astrov future are solid realities—they can hardly be that! But now I'm starting to feel as if *we're* in an uncertain state as well . . ."

"You're telling me," said Sergey.

Softly, Mikhail closed the double doors.

Osip sat in his den huddled over a sports magazine, with a half-eaten sausage and a bottle of black beer before him. He looked up.

"How's it going, then? Doesn't sound much like your ordinary sort of rehearsal to me!"

"Been listening?"

"Course I in't. Just passing the door, once in a while."

"I suppose that's why the carpet's worn threadbare."

Osip shrugged and took a swig of beer.

"We're going out," Sonya said impatiently. "We need our overcoats and galoshes."

"What you going out for?"

"For a promenade," said Mikhail. "A saunter. An ambulation. A stroll."

"All those things, eh? Shouldn't, if I were you. Can't see to spit."

"Tell me, which acting academy did *you* attend?"

Osip scratched his head. "Wonderful what rubs off on a chap, with all you artists around."

"Could we please have our things?" repeated Sonya.

Visibility was almost zero; an arm's length in any direction there was only cotton wool.

"Wonder what we'd find if we hypnotised *him*?" Mikhail jerked a gloved thumb.

"Who?"

"Osip, of course."

"You think's he's . . . ?" Sonya didn't say what.

Mikhail nodded. "He's a watchdog . . . Wonder why he lays it on so thick: the dumb pleb bit?"

"Maybe it's to give us all fair warning."

"By parodying himself? Could be."

"Maybe he likes his artists."

"Well, I don't wish to sound paranoid, my peachy psychiatrist, but if *that's* what he is, and if I do happen to be in tune with some secret research lab, I must say this could well be a field day for our friend. As soon as the phone starts working."

"Goodness, you do have a serious side, after all!"

"That's my left side, the one next to you."

Hugging close to the wall, they began walking together along the snowy path surrounding the Retreat. The white-out cocooned them.

Mikhail swept a hand through the air. "I'm beginning to believe we're all charmed . . ."

Sonya also scooped at the air, and touched the tip of a gloved finger to her tongue as though it might have picked up a curious taste.

"What *is* this: a cloud that got stuck to the ground?"

"It's a cloud of time-flakes, that's what it is. It's motes of time which haven't settled yet. Like in one of those kiddies' snow-scenes, you know? Suppose, every time you shook it, there was a new scene in the toy? Right now I'm on my way to Sakhalin . . ." He jerked his wrist. "Wait for it to settle! Ah, now I'm on my way to Tunguska . . . Try again: oh, now I'm on my way to the stars—back through history! We're fifty light years out, and Stalin's still alive. A hundred light years out, and here's the revolution." He peered into his empty hand. "Watch out: here come the wolves!"

"*What?*"

He guffawed. She could have slapped him.

"Idiot!"

They had reached the third side of the building now. From here the hard-top road had to slope away invisibly downhill. It would descend gently for the first fifty metres then much more steeply. Sonya recalled that that stretch of the road was hedged with young pine trees; so there was no way of blundering off it, even though thin snow hid the tarmac . . .

Together they ventured away from the building, sliding their galoshes ahead step by step as if they were pacing out onto a frozen lake.

After what seemed a long while, Mikhail said, "Odd! We ought to be on the slope by now, but it's still flat, ain't it?"

Nothing was visible except woolly snow and woolly fog.

86

Disoriented, Sonya almost lost her balance, but Mikhail steadied her.

"We'll be able to follow our footprints back," he reassured her. And they pressed on. He chewed his lip. "We must have reached the steep bit," he said presently.

"But we haven't."

"Look, I *know* how far it is."

"Well, so do I!"

"I'm going to try an experiment. Stay right here, Sonya. I'm going to walk off at ninety degrees till I bump into one of the trees."

"Oh no you don't."

"You'll be fine—just stand still. There ain't any Abominable Snowmen in these parts."

"Promise that you'll count up to . . . no more than twenty. Then come straight back."

"With a fir cone in my hand." Setting one foot exactly in front of the other, Mikhail vanished almost immediately. Sonya counted under her breath.

They oughtn't to have split up! She was sure of this. She lost count. She called out. Silence . . .

A second time she called his name, and strained to hear.

A hand touched her on the shoulder. Her heart lurched wildly—and then Mikhail was holding her, while she shivered and gasped.

"You bastard, that wasn't funny!" But then she saw that Mikhail looked equally surprised. "Mike, you did creep up on me, didn't you?"

"I swear I didn't! I counted to forty—okay, I'm *sorry*—and there you were just in front of me, with your back turned. No trees."

"You walked in a circle."

"I tell you I went straight."

"You must have heard me call your name."

"I heard someone call out 'Anton', twice. That ain't my

87

name—I wasn't answering to that . . . well, I got scared. Sonya, the voice was coming from *ahead* of me. And I was going to run back. then there you were."

'Did I really call "Anton"?' wondered Sonya. 'Perhaps I did . . .' She clutched hold of his arm. "What's happening to us, Mike? Where are we?"

"We're about seventy-five metres from the building. Maybe a bit more."

"But which way's *that*?" Where they stood was quite trampled in several directions. Soon, by cautious scouting around they confirmed three distinct routes: the one by which they had both come, the one Mikhail had taken on his own when he left her, and the one by which he had returned. These last two stretched in a straight line at ninety degrees to the first, forming a T-junction.

"Right," said Sonya. "We're going back."

"No." Mikhail pulled her round. "Not yet. I want to know where the hill starts. It *has* to start! We'll walk that way, where the snow's still smooth. Please, Sonya."

She hesitated. "Only thirty paces—and I'll do the counting."

"Sure. If we aren't heading downhill by then, well there just ain't no hill any more . . ."

They linked arms. "One," she began. "Two . . ."

By the time she reached eight in her count she could no longer see the ground; the fog was even denser, hiding her legs and his. When she reached twelve, she couldn't even make out Mikhail's face.

"Mike?"

"None other." He squeezed her arm. "It's easy enough to walk. No trouble breathing."

When she reached twenty, though, she could see his features emerging once again.

"Peekaboo!" he said; he didn't sound too confident.

"Twenty-one . . . Twenty-two . . ."

"Look, footsteps!"

The snow was indeed trampled—in a hauntingly familiar

fashion. And by now the fog was as it had been earlier. Only a couple of paces more, and they were back-tracking along a twin row of footsteps leading in their direction.

"Those can't be ours! Come on."

Again Sonya had lost count. But they followed the trail of footsteps onward . . . and now a wall loomed ahead of them. Mikhail ran a wondering hand over it.

"It can't be the Retreat. The Retreat's back *that way*."

"We walked in a circle."

"You know damn well we didn't."

"Look, any psychologist could tell you . . . I mean, it's so disorienting, this fog."

"The front door must be along here, round the corner."

Which it was. They hunched inside the log-pillared porch, before entering.

"What do we tell them, Mike?"

"To send Osip out, to sweep the snow."

"Be serious!"

"I mean it! With a long cord tied round his waist. We pay the string out slowly, keeping it taut . . ."

"We'd have to say why."

"True . . . In that case, there's no way we can explain."

"Isolation? Sensory deprivation?"

Mikhail squeezed Sonya round the waist. "Since you mention it, Sasha . . ."

"I am *not* Sasha Sorina." To prove this, she pecked Mikhail quickly on the cheek. Disengaging herself, she thrust the door open.

"Hang on—"

"What is it?"

"It just occurred to me, if we walk in a straight line and end up back where we started—well, do you think we could possibly phone ourselves, too?"

"Come again?"

"If a straight line leads back here, maybe the phone line does as

89

well? Let's dial the number of the Retreat and see what happens."

"That's crazy."

"So was our walk."

They surrendered their coats and galoshes to Osip who was chewing the last bite of sausage; his breath smelled of sweaty socks.

He swallowed. "Enjoy your walk, then?"

"Splendid. You should take a walk, yourself."

"Catch me, Mister!"

Mikhail grinned. "I want to use the phone."

"I told you, it isn't working."

"So maybe my magic touch will cure it?"

"Suit yourself. It's through there."

He trailed after them and hung around while Mikhail dialled; Mikhail heard a lot of clicks followed by a ringing tone.

"Hey, that's *our* number you dialled!"

"It's ringing, too." Mikhail held the hand-set for Sonya to hear.

"So it is. But nobody's answering."

"Hardly surprising—we're already here." Mikhail laid the hand-set down without bothering to cradle it. "Come on."

Osip immediately scuttled to the abandoned hand-set and scooped it up. He listened too, then cradled it hastily and pursued Mikhail and Sonya to the door to see them off his premises.

Mikhail sauntered a few paces down the corridor before stopping to fuss with his shoe. "Damned lace!"

As soon as he heard the door close, he tiptoed back to eavesdrop. Straining, he heard the whirr of Osip dialling a new number— followed by a bewildered curse and the slam of the hand-set being banged down. Grinning, he caught up with Sonya.

"That's given him food for thought."

"Us too, Mike. Us too." She pushed open the double doors.

"Ah, Mr Petrov," Kirilenko called out heartily. "Refreshed, and ready for another bout?"

Seventeen

LYDIA-POPOVA THREW the revolver down on the table. It was Anton's own revolver, commandeered for the occasion. An embroidered linen tablecloth concealed a thick felt underlay, thus protecting Governor Vladimirov's precious rosewood from any scars or dents.

"My fingers are stiff from holding the horrid thing!" In a transport of fury she began twisting her lace handkerchief as though to massage life back into her hand. "Why are you standing there?" she shouted at Vershinin-Smirnov. "Get out!"

Meanwhile Anton regarded the proceedings quizzically from the very back of the huge reception room. Crystal chandeliers blazed and the heavy tasselled curtains were closed, though there was still ample daylight outside. Twenty rows of chairs, upholstered in maroon velvet, seated the cream of local society. A number of the men—notably the Governor—wore military uniform; others were dressed in frock coats; but quite a few lounged in shabbier duds. One fellow was puffing a cigar; beside him an old buffer in dundreary whiskers was snoozing. Of the ladies, some wore old-fashioned crinolettes, and others had their skirts tied back tightly under their buttocks; there were also gowns with high collars and flounced shoulders. A few of the women were wagging Chinese fans.

And every few moments the whole audience would burst into a cacophony of laughter, which drowned the dialogue—the men slapping their sides to stop them splitting; so presumably this performance of *The Bear* could be regarded as a huge success . . .

The hoots and guffaws lanced through Anton's head like

migraine. 'Dear God,' he thought, 'isn't people's taste appalling?'

"I love you!" Vershinin bellowed. "This is the last thing in the world I need! I've got that interest to pay off tomorrow. The haymaking's just started. And now there's you!"

When he seized Lydia round the waist, the watching women's eyes popped with delighted scandal.

He wailed, "I'll never forgive myself!" And the audience convulsed.

"You just keep away from me!" cried Lydia. "Take your hands off! I loathe you!" She reached towards the revolver . . . but she didn't pick it up. "I . . . I challenge you!"

"Bravo!" the cigar puffer cried.

And suddenly Lydia and Vershinin fell into each other's arms and kissed . . . and kissed . . . and carried on smooching passionately for an inordinately long time. Rodé seemed to have missed his cue. Or maybe he was delaying his entry out of mischief. The audience oooh-ed and aaah-ed.

At long last Rodé did bustle in, waving an axe. He was followed by several extras recruited from among the Governor's own servants. These men were a little uncertain as to what was actually going on, and visibly nervous to be hauling gardening tools into the best room in the house. But this was all part of the fun. The spectators cackled at the gardener with his rake and the coachman with a pitchfork in his hand and the other workmen wielding spades as cudgels.

"Holy Saints!" shrieked Rodé as he caught sight of Lydia and Vershinin locked in an embrace.

Lydia contrived to look demure. With eyes downcast, she delivered her punch line. "Looka, you can tell them that Toby isn't to have *any* oats today!" So much for her recently deceased husband's favourite horse . . .

And that was that. Since there was no curtain—except for the curtains at the windows—Lydia, Vershinin and Rodé all stood stock still for a few moments, before stepping forward in unison, Lydia to curtsey, the two men to bow deeply from the waist.

92

The audience burst into applause—and the extras milled about in confusion, till Vershinin noticed and chased them gruffly off. Fleeing, the servants crushed through the doorway in a pack, and the rake got jammed across it . . .

Some wit cried out, "Author!" Turning about in their seats, everyone took up the call. Anton rose reluctantly, and bowed.

"Speech!"

"No, please . . ." He spread his hands beseechingly. "All the credit belongs to our fine actors."

Rodé brandished the axe aloft. "Not a speech about *this*! A speech about the expedition!"

"Absolutely so!" seconded the bewhiskered gentleman—who had recovered consciousness the moment the play was over. "To the front with you, man!"

During Anton's speech, Lydia passed blithely amongst the audience bearing a collecting bowl—which, a little later, she announced had netted a thousand roubles. Once again—what a farce, in both senses!—*The Bear* had bailed Anton out . . .

Servants carried the chairs aside to clear the floor for dancing and drinking; and a buffet was wheeled in. Immediately half the men made a bee line for it.

Gaily Lydia handed Anton's gun back to him. "Come and chat with the Governor, Anton Pavlovich! Looka!" she called to Rodé, "*do* get rid of that axe. You look like a madman."

'Looka,' indeed? So Lydia was still carrying on the drama in her head? Either it was the sign of the great actress, or a mono-maniac . . .

Three musicians arrived, bearing fiddles and a guitar. 'Surely I don't have to dance!' thought Anton. 'I'll be the bear, then. I'll be the capering, baited bear . . .'

The original bear, Vershinin, was deep in converse with Governor Vladimirov. Lydia tugged at Anton's sleeve, and he pocketed the gun hastily as she drew him towards the Governor, to join in . . .

How many fathers or grandfathers of people in this very room had once similarly skulked towards someone in authority, with a weapon or a petition or an incriminating letter concealed about their person? It occurred to him that *Exiles* might be a good title for a comedy . . . or perhaps not. Even if it was a knock-about farce, with a title like that it probably hadn't a cat in Hell's chance of passing the Censor . . . Still, it could make a publishable story—something to give the lie to all those smart brats at *Russian Idea* with their beady, liberal eyes trained remorselessly on Mr Chekhov . . . Was this any way for an honest writer to think?

As he waited his turn to speak, nostalgia overwhelmed him. He yearned for a summerhouse overlooking a little orchard, rather than the infinite forests hereabouts. Yes, with a good fishing stream nearby instead of a raging Siberian torrent . . .

But any summerhouse he bought would probably turn out to be riddled with woodworm; and the trees in the orchard would suffer from blight . . . Yet the stream, ah the stream! He could sit on its bank for hours on end with a rod in his hand, while the world and life degenerated all about him until the cold death of everything . . .

Surely there must be an orchard somewhere! For that matter, the whole world could be an orchard one day . . . 'What a hope,' he thought. And yet he hoped.

The Governor clapped a hand on him.

"Anton Pavlovich, I haven't laughed so much for ages! You must tell me the secret of your comic talent . . ."

Eighteen

ANTON ASTROV STOPPED whistling the Czarist anthem a few seconds before 3.00 p.m., Moscow time. "*Now*, Anna."

And Anna Aksakova pressed the button to begin their Flux-jump; they started to fall through time . . .

Alarm bells rang out immediately; red lights stabbed on and off. Stars frisked about on the viewscreens. The Moon raced from one screen to the next, trailing phosphorescence in its wake.

On the central screen the image of Earth held steady, but all detail had disappeared: the world blurred and foamed like a whisking bowl.

Sasha pointed a shaky finger at the frothing Earth. "Why are we still here? Why hasn't it gone?"

Anton quickly shut off all the bells and panic-lights. "Here? Where *is* here, anyway? Yuri?"

Valentin consulted the retardograph and temporal symptomometer. "Time minus 5 years. T minus 5.3 . . . minus 5.7 . . . We're diving backwards through time, all right! If you can call it diving. Drifting, more like."

"The Earth's spinning backwards," Sasha said. "We're seeing it speeded up—that's why it's so blurred."

"And yet we've left the present," said Yuri Valentin. "T minus 6.8 . . ."

"But we should be light years away by now," said Anton.

"Well, we aren't. We're following the world-line exactly."

They all stared at the Earth spinning widdershins on the screen.

Presently Yuri tapped a jagged graph displayed on the cathode screen of the chronodyne resonometer.

"Resonance, that's it! Look, here's the evidence. The instant our own flux-field went into action, so did a second flux-field. The two fields resonated momentarily. This had the effect of subtracting most of our spatial momentum. We got glued to the Earth's world-line, kilometre for kilometre, year for year."

"A second flux-field?"

"It must have been Captain America's Shield switching on, Commander."

"Was it deliberate? Did they try to sabotage us?"

"Spontaneous, I'd say. There must be an acausal trigger effect, independent of distance . . ." Yuri pointed at the isocalendar. "Look, our temporal momentum got slowed as well. This'll affect our point of emergence in past time—it could shake it plus or minus fifty years."

"Are you sure it wasn't malicious?"

"No, the other flux-field switched on the *very instant* ours did—without even a nanosecond's delay! No human skill could have arranged it. And I can tell you, if it *was* intentional it was a bloody stupid thing to do. Time-energy must have been transferred."

"To the Earth?"

"Presumably."

"Well, what effect would that have?"

Yuri shook his head. "I'm not a time-theorist—nobody on board is. Those types all stayed behind at their cushy research jobs in Academgorodok and Krasnoyarsk. We're star-colonists; so what do we need to know about time-theory?"

"We *were* star-colonists. Right now it looks as though we'll end up colonising the Earth—a century or two ago."

Sasha unbuckled herself. "You forget Cosmic Censorship. Paradox isn't allowed. I'm going to take a naked eyeball look." She drifted up towards the observation pod.

"Be careful! It could be damned disorienting, seeing all this in the raw."

"It's my job, Commander." Sasha disappeared through the hatch.

Anton turned to Anna. "What's your opinion of the consequences, Earth-wise?"

"How do I know? Time-storms, maybe?"

"What are time-storms, Aksakova? Come on, tell me. Are they like snow-storms?"

"How do I know what they're like? Or even if such things can happen? It's just a word—to cover our ignorance."

"T minus 15.5 years," said Yuri.

At T minus 25 years Sasha bobbed back through the hatch; catching hold of Anton's seat, she righted herself.

"Rough, up there?"

"Of course it's bad . . . That isn't the worst thing!" Scrambling to her own seat, she fiddled with the radar. "I thought so—we're diving towards the Earth. We're on collision course."

"Oh shit. How long have we got left?"

"How many years till it happens, that's the important thing," said Yuri. "Not how many minutes ahead, but how many years *ago*. Sasha, patch yourself into my console and we'll try to compute it."

"But this ship can't possibly enter the Earth's atmosphere," said Anna. "We aren't aerodynamic."

"Oh, we can enter the atmosphere all right," snapped Anton. "What happens then is another matter."

Anna hesitated. "The flux-field might protect us . . . as though we're in an envelope. I mean, we aren't in direct contact with our own space-time environment, are we? We're only in virtual contact."

"Oh yes. But can we navigate, while we're in virtual contact? Well, maybe we can, at that! Anna, I want you to fire the starboard and upper attitude jets—then light the plasma torch."

She swallowed. "Acknowledged. Five seconds, and counting . . ."

Five seconds later the ship jerked and shuddered; but the central screen remained full of the Earth, swirling amorphously.

"This isn't normal motion that's taking us in," said Anna hopelessly. "It's the Flux."

"Any chance of killing the field?"

"Before the pre-set time? I'd have to reprogramme."

"How long would that take?"

"By the looks of it: too long."

"Start doing it, anyway—conditions may alter. Yuri, any idea what year we'll hit the Earth?"

Valentin had been trying to average the fluctuating readings of his datalscope. "I think it'll be some time between 1910 and 1908."

"Where, geographically, Sorina?"

"Possibly it'll be . . . where we were looking at before Anna pushed the button."

"The Indian Ocean? Himalayas? Suppose we re-enter there . . . we end up over . . . *Siberia.*"

"I'd say the best estimate is 1908."

"1908? My God. That was the year of the Tunguska explosion! Are *we* the Tunguska event?"

Anna sat back. "If so, then we've had it. Because Tunguska already *happened*—we can't alter that, can we?"

"Tunguska might have been something else: a giant meteor, anything. Carry on trying!"

"Or it might have been the first and last flux-ship from the future . . ."

"T minus 37 years."

Nineteen

AT LONG LAST—and none too soon for Anton's liking, since he was heartily fed up with Krasnoyarsk by now—on a crisp blue Thursday the expedition was ready to set off, from a jetty on the Yenisey. (The weather was also ready for them: mornings were sharp with frost again, and flurries of snow had blown by during the past few days.)

Scores of well-wishers and spectators gathered on the riverbank; foremost among them Governor Vladimirov and his lady, accompanied by the editor of *Krasnoyarets* who had written an extolling leader the day before. Rodé and Fedotik were there, of course, though they too would quit Krasnoyarsk within hours; they had received further travel expenses and testy orders to proceed post-haste to the Amur before the full onset of winter could entrap them into months of gambling, balls and other festivities.

Old Polena and Olga Franzovna were shepherding Lydia's daughters . . .

Masha waved and wept and capered, and at one point was in danger of falling into the river. But Nastya squinted tightly at her Mother, as though Countess Lydia was a criminal who ought to be reported for abandoning her family, were it not for the amazing fact that the authorities connived corruptly in whatever was going on. The little girl stared daggers at Vershinin—to get rid of him; though this was useless, since he seemed to be *eloping* with her Mother. And Mr Chekhov she continued to regard with beady suspicion. He was supposed to be famous, but he didn't behave as if he believed it; so Nastya suspected a confidence trick—particularly when Mama had given the man so much money. Mr Chekhov hadn't even shown a scrap of interest in his 'own' play! Maybe he hadn't actually written it . . . As for that scruffy fellow Tsiolkovsky, whom the said 'Chekhov' had invited once he'd tested the bath-water with his toe, obviously *he* was a shady accomplice! None of his hamstrung, hectic talk of people on other planets and ships sailing through the sky had fooled little Nastya. It was simply amazing how gullible grown-ups could be.

In one respect the girl was looking forward to her Mama's absence with some relish. For this would allow her ample leeway to practise deceptions of her own—upon silly Masha, and daft old Polena. Maybe even upon dear Olga Franzovna, too—though Nastya respected that effervescent lady's ability to make cards vanish and pop up in unexpected places. Still, a governess was only a jumped-up servant!

Finally, Nastya brought herself to wave. And a moment later, to her great surprise, she also cried.

The six members of the expedition had embarked upon two specially constructed rafts, piloted by a small gang of hired rivermen. Stout rails penned the pack horses with their stock of hay, two sledges, and assorted panniers, saddlebags and boxes. On the first raft rode Sidorov, Mirek and Tsiolkovsky; on the second, Vershinin, Lydia Zelenina and Anton.

As the rivermen poled them away from the jetty into the rushing current, Lydia snapped a photograph of all the people waving farewell then restored her camera to the safety of its waterproof box.

"Well, the die is cast," said Vershinin. "Or as Vasily Romanych would put it: the Rubicon is crossed!"

"But we aren't crossing the Yenisey," Lydia said, puzzled. "Not till we get to the Angara . . ."

"Exactly!" Vershinin roared with laughter. "But that's what old Fedotik would say, bless his heart."

She smiled at him. "Yes, he would, wouldn't he?"

Meanwhile Fedotik and everyone else on the shore diminished swiftly in size till they were indistinguishable. Anton turned away, and began to roll a cigarette. Had Krasnoyarsk been Moscow itself, he would still have been bored with it long ago . . .

This first stage of the route was by far the easiest: swiftly downstream along the river for a couple of hundred versts as far as the confluence with the Angara. Soon they left the lumber mills and tanneries and workers' hovels behind; and then, behind them too, some chilly marshes where the honk of geese sounded more like the sad croaking of frogs soon to be interred by ice. Presently, forest pressed gloomily about both banks.

Occasionally their rafts sped past a clearing in the mass of spruce and stone pine, larch and silver fir; there would be a hut or two, where a few peasants might be hunched around a wood fire, smoking fish to last them through the winter. Once or twice they passed a vaster devastated scab, work of one of the summer's forest fires. But these gaps in the woodland were as nothing.

"All these trees!" exclaimed Lydia effervescently. "What a theme for drama!"

"Do you really think so?" asked Vershinin. "Surely there's no action in trees—you need action in a drama, eh Anton Pavlovich?"

For weeks now Anton had suspected it would be a wise move never to write another play again . . .

"You do agree, don't you?"

"If you say so, Nikolai."

Lydia struck a poetic pose. While the rivermen gaped at her, she improvised:

"Surely the Angel of Silence has passed over this land! With her wing she has brushed the ducks, the herons, the hares, the . . . the frozen mammoths slumbering in the soil, and the infinitude of trees. How fearful is this silence! Heaven help the homeless wayfarer lost in it!

"Yet the humblest human wayfarer is a Higher Being. He is higher than a goose or a fox. Wherever *he* goes, in his despair, he

101

seeks—all unknowing—for the World Soul of the taiga . . . to free her from that seal of silence so that she shall finally speak her secrets—hidden from all human ears and eyes till now."

Vershinin grinned. "I thought we were looking for a million tons of iron . . . or a shipwreck from the stars?"

"And only she, the World Soul, knows where those brave Higher Beings from the heavens have found their last resting place . . . Kolya."

"Tsiolkovsky says they all evaporated into thin air."

"Ah, but what if they didn't? Just imagine, Kolya, finding the body of a being even higher than Mankind! It would be like coming upon the corpse of an angel . . . preserved by the cold, the way the mammoths are preserved. Imagine a play written about a Baron—who gets exiled to Siberia for conspiracy. He escapes! And he's trudging through the wilderness in despair, soliloquizing, when suddenly he finds the dead body of an angel . . . Or maybe the World Soul herself hears him and crosses his path. She guides him through this army of trees to where the angel lies . . . And lo!" Lydia gestured. "Here she comes! Behold the World Soul, herself!"

Just then another little clearing happened to open on the riverbank; wrapped in a shawl of rags a crone stood staring blankly over the rushing water at them.

With a chuckle, Anton tossed his latest spent cigarette away. "You really ought to write that play when we get back, Lydia Fyodorovna."

"Should I? Ah, the words flow freely enough at the moment—but how does one halt them for long enough to set them down?" Lydia clapped her hands. "I know! I shall dictate the speeches to Olga, while I walk around composing them. She'll be my amanuensis."

For a while the rivermen had been humming to themselves. Now the humming grew louder, like a hive of bees. Before long they struck up a dirge of a song. It was about the great bell of Uglich, deported across the Urals to Siberian Tobolsk for the crime of having been rung by rebels. This had happened four centuries ago, yet the memory of that ancient banishment was still as freshly preserved as a prehistoric carcase by the perma-frost . . .

Twenty

AND STILL THE white-out wrapped the Retreat . . .

"Oh, and let's not forget how Konstantin Fucking Tsiolkovsky is bound to invent the Geiger counter just as soon as he gets to Tunguska! Do I really have to be the amanuensis of this rot? Why don't we just collar a couple of bottles and all get pissed?"

"I do sympathise," Felix said to Sergey, "but why don't you look at it this way: suppose we were to scrap the original scheme for the film—?"

"Are you as barmy as he is?"

"Half a tick! Just listen. Suppose we made a different film—*namely*, this other film which Mikhail is handing us on a plate. It could be highly original, very imaginative! It would put our names on the map: as Soviet artists of the first calibre."

"It could just as easily land us all in jail—if some Physics boffin in Academgorodok or Krasnoyarsk, unquote, happens to be scribbling secret equations for 'time-flux' travel!"

"Oh, I hardly think that's very likely. Don't forget, too: this new film would be anti-Imperialist—the Americans only use their time technology for military purposes. Whereas *we* use it to colonise the cosmos. Then their Shield buggers up everyone's hopes of the stars and causes the Tunguska explosion instead. It could be a rather cutting parable." Felix turned to Kirilenko. "What d'you think, Victor Alexeyevich?"

Kirilenko was appalled. "But this would present the split-hypnosis technique in entirely the wrong light! It would show the subject splitting into two separate fantasy personae! No, no."

"So what do you suggest? We scrap the whole project—after

running our Chekhov Look-Alike Contest? We'd be a laughing stock. I say we should make the *very best* of what's happened—and we'll knock everyone sideways with it."

"I think we ought to get pissed," said Sergey. "Perhaps we'll see our way out through the bottom of a glass, or six. *In vodka veritas!*—or is that your sort of line, Petrov?"

Mikhail ignored him. He was glancing from the cotton wool outside the window to Sonya, and back, as though to prompt her.

"And what's the climax of this new film, pray?"

"I've no doubt Mikhail will tell us presently. As soon as he finds out himself."

"Don't suppose the old story matters very much! Pretty stupid idea, really! Kind of simple-minded, eh? What sort of blockhead could ever have dreamed it up?"

"Please!" said Felix. "This'll be an experimental film . . . and it'll be a thoroughly committed one into the bargain."

"Committed? It's us lot who ought to be committed—to the nearest nut-house!" Sergey glared at Kirilenko. "Oops, the nut-house is here already." He jumped up. "I refuse to have any more to do with this farcical distortion of an honest project—into sheer fantasy. I'm walking out, in fact. Right now."

"But you can't," Mikhail said softly.

"Oh, so now he's the bloody script-writer and security man and everyone else!"

Sonya hesitated, then nodded to Mikhail. "Yes, go on: tell them."

Mikhail spoke in a jolly way. "Well, I'm sorry to spoil your weekend, Sergey old son, but it's physically impossible to get *away* from this place. When we went out for our little walk a while back, Sonya and I tried to go down the hill—and we found ourselves right back here where we started. I might add, we were walking in a perfectly straight line, too!"

"What, cuddling and smooching and you had time to watch where you were walking?"

Sonya started up, as though to slap him. "I suggest," she said icily, "you try it yourself, Mr Pig."

"Oh, I shall." Sergey hauled out of his pocket the keys to the Film Unit's battered old Volga, garaged round the back of the building.

"You'll end up in a ditch," said Felix. "And where does that leave the rest of us, if you run off with the car?"

"I'm sure you'll amuse yourselves adequately—"

"Sergey, I *won't* be bullied. We need to explore this other option—let's keep an open mind, eh? We could revert to your idea later on."

Sergey jingled the keys. "Nothing doing."

Felix pursed his lips. "How very egocentric."

"Quite the prima donna," Sonya gladly added.

"Okay. Look, damn it: I've been challenged, haven't I?" Sergey flushed. "So I'll drive down the hill, and I'll find somewhere to report our phone out of order. Then I'll drive straight back up here again, right? I swear to you, either I get out of this madhouse for a breather—or I hit the bottle! Preferably on top of Mikhail's skull. In fact, if I don't leave this minute I'm going to throw up."

"Perhaps a little hypnosis could help you?" Kirilenko pointed placatingly at the dusty sofa.

"Fuck off with your hypnosis." Sergey wrenched the doors open, and fled.

Kirilenko went over to close the doors. "I do seem to recall that having me here was *his* idea in the first place . . ."

"How can I apologize properly?"

Kirilenko shrugged Felix's excuses away. "I think Sergey's notion of having a stiff drink wasn't a bad one at all." He wandered across to the window, but there was nothing whatever to be seen from it.

"First rate idea! Mike, tell Osip to dig out a bottle and some glasses, will you?"

Mikhail chuckled. "Won't it look as though we're having a party to celebrate his absence?"

"Who cares?" Sonya said. "Besides, he's going to need a stiff drink as soon as he gets back."

"He will?" asked Kirilenko.

"Because he isn't going to be able to drive down that hill. Because right now it *isn't there*."

"Now, now, Sonya, you know full well that the mind plays tricks on itself when there's reduced sensory input. Why, the very basis of hypnosis—"

Kirilenko didn't finish, nor did Mikhail even reach the doors on his errand—for these burst open, and in stumbled Osip, grey with fright.

He headed for Felix. "I have to talk to you, Comrade!"

"What's wrong, man? The car hasn't crashed already, has it?"

"Car, what car? I managed to phone out, that's what's wrong. See, I been testing the phone every now and then."

"I bet you have," said Mikhail. "Who did you get: yourself?"

Osip stared round, uncomprehending. "I dialled . . . somebody I know. But the guy on the other end was a total stranger. 'Who gave you this number?' he wants to know. And: 'What you calling me for, on a Sunday?' 'Eh, Comrade,' says I, reasonable-like, 'it's only Saturday afternoon.' So he starts in threatening and heaping abuse and calling me a saboteur and a silly joker—and next he says OGPU'll sort out the likes of me. I ask you: OGPU! That's years and years ago."

Muffled by double glazing and the fog, they heard the engine of the Volga revving, choke full out . . .

"You sure, Osip?"

"Sure as eggs is eggs, Mr Levin. He said OGPU."

"He was having you on."

"Not on that number, he wasn't."

They heard the car drive off very slowly; perhaps there was a faint glow from its headlights, perhaps not.

"Dear old Osip." Mikhail draped an arm about the caretaker, almost affectionately. "Join the club."

"What club's that, then? What's going on here? You two used

the phone! You called our own number—I saw you! What did you do that for?"

"To see if it would ring. It did."

"Is that true?" Kirilenko asked Sonya. "You mean you phoned the same phone you were using—and you got it? That's impossible."

"And Osip phoned out," she said, "and he got somebody years and years ago, long before the KGB were even dreamed of. I think we can all avoid asking Osip *why* he was phoning his favourite number."

"Yup," said Mikhail. "We're all in the same boat now. We're riding out the time-storm."

"What the devil are you two talking about?" Felix cried.

"Well, it's what Sonya and I discovered on our little stroll together . . ." Mikhail cupped a hand behind his ear. "Aha, and here he comes driving back, I do believe! Now, won't he be surprised?"

"Oughtn't it to be getting dark?" Kirilenko consulted his watch. "Heavens, it ought to be black dark! Ah—our lights must be illuminating the fog. Weird effect."

"No night, nor day," murmured Sonya. "Not any more—time's gone away . . ."

Somewhere around the corner, outside, a car engine roared and died.

"You know," said Mikhail to her, "that means there isn't any secret funny business going on in Physics labs. The centre of this thing's right here. It's in this building. It's us—it's what we're doing."

Feet came running down the hallway; Sergey appeared in the door. His eyes bulged, as if he'd met a ghost in a graveyard.

"It won't go down—"

"What won't, the Volga?"

"The bloody hill won't go down! It isn't there—I nearly drove into this building! Had to jump on the brakes, I did."

Mikhail grinned. "You couldn't by any chance have skidded

108

round in a full circle? No, I suppose not . . ." He relented. "Sorry, old man—excuse my mockery! Osip, be a good chap and fetch us a bottle of vodka? We all need a drink. You do, too—come and join us."

"How come I couldn't drive away?" bleated Sergey.

"Ain't anywhere to drive *to*. There ain't anything out there at the moment. We can't leave till it's all over."

Sergey subsided into an armchair.

With extraordinary dispatch, Osip fairly bustled in only a few moments later bearing a tray of glasses, with two half-litre bottles of Stolichnaya hooked between his fingers. Crashing the tray on to the table, he tore the caps off both bottles and poured shakily. Sergey hauled himself up, sniffing and snorting like a camel approaching an oasis. Perhaps this was just to clear the white fog from his nostrils. Or it might have been to stop himself from bursting into tears . . .

Twenty-one

"PRESUMABLY I'D BETTER tell the crew," said Commander Astrov.

"Why tell them we're all doomed? What can *they* do about it? You'll only spread panic."

"Yuri's right," said Sasha.

"But I told them the time-jump would be quasi-instantaneous—so why haven't I announced that we've emerged? They're probably worried sick already. Do you think they didn't notice the ship bucking like a horse when Anna fired the jets?"

"So we've been *busy*! We're trying to avoid space junk at the other end. T minus 43 years," Yuri added more calmly with a glance at his retardograph. "Look, there's no time to launch our shuttles—even if they could break out of the flux-field, which I doubt."

"I'm sure everyone ought to be told. It's an awful thing to go to your death ignorantly."

"Thanks, but I'd rather be taken by surprise—right out of the blue."

"Oh, it's out of the blue *we'll* be coming in a few more minutes, and no mistake! I wonder if anyone in Siberia looked up in the sky and saw a Hammer and Sickle flying down from space? A sort of vision of future time . . . Maybe some of the reindeer people saw it. The Evenki . . . Then all the trees were knocked flat—just the way Czarist society was knocked flat a few years later . . . Shit, this is absurd talk. I'm going to tell them. How's the reprogramming coming on?"

"Slowly," said Anna Aksakova.

Yuri spoke up, more to delay Anton than for any other reason. "You do realize, don't you Commander, that the flux-field is going to have to hold steady till almost the very end? Otherwise, given our shape, we'd be torn to pieces by the atmosphere and scattered across half of Asia. But we weren't. I mean: we won't be."

"Yes, that figures. We have to return to the Earth, our home . . . I wonder if it's actually impossible to get away from our world by using the time-flux? Have you thought of that, Yuri?"

"How do you mean?"

"Oh, we can send as much dead matter to the stars as we like—or as far back in time as we want. But as soon as we try to send conscious, living beings, it doesn't work . . . What *is* time? Nobody really knows."

Yuri pretended interest. "Surely the main point is that all equations for physical processes work just as well in reverse as forwards? So processes can occur in either time-direction— theoretically. Well, we've proved that in practice, haven't we?" He indicated his console. "T minus 47, see?" Immediately he regretted his gesture; he ought to be keeping the Commander's mind *off* their impending doom.

"Ah, but your equations don't tell us what time *is*."

"Surely it has to do with the entropy total," Yuri said cautiously.

"But what if it doesn't? What if the 'passage' of time is a construct of consciousness—of *evolving* consciousness? Maybe that's why time seems to flow from past to future. Maybe it's because of the dynamics of our evolution. And where, pray, did we evolve?" Anton stabbed a finger towards the main viewscreen, filled with the wild, solid fog which was part of the Earth. "Right down there, where else? Maybe 'time' as we know it doesn't exist elsewhere in the universe. Because time hasn't been constructed— out there. So we can't get away from Earth by travelling through time."

"Surely not! What happened to the test probes we sent through the Flux? They certainly didn't turn up on an earlier Earth, or

111

people would have found them years ago. They were rigged to transmit for a hundred years."

"Maybe they just . . . stopped existing?"

"Things don't just cease to exist," said Sasha sharply. "The Law of Conservation forbids it."

"*We'll* soon cease to exist, Astrogator."

"Oh no we won't! We will turn into heat and light and particles and droplets of germanium and copper and everything else. But the sum total of mass and energy won't stop existing!"

"Have you ever looked at a table of geological eras, Sorina?"

"Of course. Hasn't everybody?"

"Yes, they look. But they don't notice . . . one little detail. Each successive era is *shorter* than the one before—a child could plot the shrinking on a graph."

"Shrinking?"

"That's what I said. Look, the Carboniferous era lasts for about 350 million years. The Permian lasts for 280. Next comes the Triassic, at 230. Then there's the Jurassic, at 190. And so on. Getting shorter all the time."

"But that's just a convenient way of dividing prehistory."

"Is it indeed? I'll tell you what it is. As life and brain structures evolve, so does time *speed up*. First of all, it's all very slow and stately—but lately it's been zipping along."

"That's . . . preposterous."

"I thought you'd say so. And meanwhile, *tempus fugit* for us too . . ." Anton switched on his chin-mike. "Commander Astrov to All Crew: hear this . . . !"

"No!" Yuri whispered urgently. "Maybe you're right about the geological eras. Maybe nobody else ever put two and two together—"

"Shut up, Yuri . . .

". . . We have met unexpected difficulties, Comrades. We have failed to leave Earthspace. We are currently proceeding backwards through time at a rate of approximately three years per ship minute. However, we are also closing in on the planet Earth at considerable speed. You will have noticed our evasive manoeuvres. These proved unsuccessful. Chief Engineer Aksakova is reprogramming our flight pattern to bring us out of flux prematurely, before we impact with the atmosphere. I shall keep you informed. Be brave, Comrades."

The *K. E. Tsiolkovsky* continued plummeting through time, back towards its world of origin . . .

Twenty-two

My wonderful Masha, beloved Mama,
and everyone else at home,
Goodness only knows when (or from where) this letter will ever be posted! Perhaps it isn't really a letter at all, but a journal? Destined for your own sweet eyes, dear Sister, when I return home again . . .

If so, I haven't the foggiest how to proceed! For whom does one address in this kind of 'diary of the heart'? One's own heart, perhaps?

All I know about my own heart is that it keeps on beating steadily—thump, thump—despite the awful struggles of the last week and more.

I suppose you really address the future in such a piece of scribbling as a 'private journal'. You're full of egotistical hopes that this vague entity, Futurity, will disinter all your carefully orchestrated secrets from the desk drawer where you've hidden them—leaving the key in the lock, of course! Whereupon eager Futurity will at once declare what a fascinating chap this Anton Pavlovich Chekhov was. And it'll all be a big bluff.

How can I sum up the sequence of days since we quit the Yenisey for our long tramp, 350 versts eastwards, along the banks of the Angara?

Well, there was already enough light snow cover this far north for us to use the sledges, as we'd counted on doing. And that meant fighting our way through branches quite a lot of the time. (I have scratches and cuts all over my mug, as if I've been whipped by invisible forest spirits wielding tiny lashes.) And sometimes we were forced to take to the shallows of the river to haul the sledges upstream some way, which involved a lot of skidding and stumbling and getting dunked in icy water. We have shivered around camp fires—about which I can assure you there's nothing romantic. Wild ducks and geese have avoided our guns with great dexterity, save for a couple of scraggy specimens potted by Countess Lydia. Sidorov managed to net one salmon-trout, but otherwise I'd hardly describe the Angara as an angler's paradise—the fish didn't seem to know what the game was about. So all in all this has amounted to a disturbing lack of victuals from the land. No hares, no bears or giant rats. Not even any tigers.

Just trees. Trees, trees, was the long and the short of it: an infinity of snow-dusted spruce, frosted larch and silver fir. And every day more snow fell, gently and persistently, muffling the world—till it seemed as though our colour vision was failing through disuse, and the whole planet had turned white. Often even the air was white with freezing fog.

We passed through a few little human settlements, but on the whole there wasn't a living thing to be seen. Apart from the motion of the river—flowing in the wrong direction—it appeared that life had shut up shop for ever. Oh the silence—it haunts you! The taiga steals away every sound, till you fear you've gone deaf as well as blind. And so you mumble to yourself . . .

Bah, the idiotic joy we felt when we sighted the scurvy huts of Zaimskove a few days back. You'd think we'd arrived outside the walls of Babylon, or seen Monsieur Eiffel's modern wonder looming on the horizon. Oh to renew acquaintance with a bed-bug! Oh to meet a cockroach on a wall! The experience was positively metropolitan.

And now at last we're in Kezhma, where the Tungusi from the north trade their furs in the spring. Almost all the roofs of this fine city are made of sods. Of streets there are exactly two and a half, and these peter out very quickly.

But on the subject of Tungusi, we have been lucky enough to hire a guide . . .

This fellow, Tolya by naine, has apparently been hanging around Kezhma for the past five or six months, doing odd jobs on what pass for farms in the vicinity instead of tramping off smartly back to his family tents deep in the wilderness. Perhaps he has been trying to become an example of Urban Man? But he looks like an Eskimo, and speaks Russian accordingly.

Ach, I suppose it's all a question of degree! If this Tungusi specimen is Russianized, just so are we Russians . . . Europeanized! We all remain slovenly Asiatics at heart . . .

We'll certainly be glad of his local knowledge on the next stretch of the journey. For here at Kezhma is where we strike off overland through the virgin taiga, heading for the trading post of Vanavara a hundred versts away on the southerly branch of the Stony Tunguska.

Tonight the snow flakes are drifting down again. And I think I must be crazy to be stuck out in this back of beyond when I could already be home, near to you, dear Masha, with all my research on Sakhalin over and done with!

Am I crazy? It's easy to take leave of one's senses in these parts. I've mentioned how people mumble to themselves: often it's the same word or phrase repeated over and over a thousand times, as if this is the key to the meaning of life. You get a bee in your bonnet, and it buzzes round all day till its humming is the only sound you can hear in the whole world.

My own particular foible, as I found out after five or six days of sledging and tramping, was to perceive every tree I passed—as a book, bound in bark! For what else are books, but trees in another form? I became quite obsessed with the idea. Here was I, travelling through all my past and future works, set out in a uniform edition. And as regards originality, no book differed by a jot from any other! This one might be called *The Spruce* and the one after, *The Stone Pine*—and the one after that, *The Larch*. But they would all amount to the same thing: another damn tree! Instead of, say, a skylark—or an elephant. Or a dragon. Oh, the ennui of it!

Old Grigorovich told me to write a novel . . . But, dear me, the characters I dreamed up are all moribund. The fine women I envisaged are wrinkled and senile by now: their skins as coarse and rutted as the bark of these wretched trees . . .

But here's the real nightmare: supposing this trek into the wilderness was a novel in its own right? What persons do I have in it? Why, exactly the sort of people whom I faithfully promised myself never to write about! There's Countess Lydia—a 'new' type of woman. There's a 'superfluous man'—old Sidorov (reinvigorated but still, I fear, condemned). And there's a het-up, pedantic visionary: Konstantin Eduardovich, no less . . .

Of course, I do Tsiolkovsky an injustice! But really, when I hear him going on about the ecstasy of escaping the bondage of gravity and flitting about in free space, my ears detect such a strident metaphor for our own social conditions in Russia. I can already hear all the intellectual lackeys taking up this refrain in a chorus—and completely ignoring what life is really like. They'll get up a subscription to build Tsiolkovsky a rocket, which might blow him to pieces, and meanwhile they'll ignore an outbreak of cholera in their own back yard . . .

Oh, these pilgrimages that we Russians devote our lives to! Is this one any different? Off we march to the holy scientific icon of Tunguska, to unswaddle our souls, and prostrate ourselves before a mystery!

Masha, I must pull myself together. I'm sure we haven't any real hope of solving the mystery awaiting us. We'd be hotheads to try to! The evidence is what matters. We must gather a portfolio of evidence—then I can escape from all this, and get on boring the public with *The Stone Pine* or whatever. (I don't think I'll write a comedy about 'The Exiled Baron and the World Soul'! But that's another story . . .)

Of course, if I did put my literary scruples aside and wrote a novel of adventure, well, I could have a gruff but romantic Baron, a dashing Countess conducting an adulterous liaison in her tent—we'll overlook the fact that she's already a widow, shall we? And then there's our home-bred Russian Hamlet, Sidorov, equipped with a bold quest to take his mind off suicide. . . We mustn't forget our noble savage, Tolya, either—how does he fit in? Will he give his life for us, fighting off a hungry bear? (And I don't mean Baron Vershinin!)

Ah, if it were a novel, what trash it would be! And what a popular success! I can see the reviews already. '*A real change of pace for Mr Chekhov: Bravo!*' '*On the other hand, fellow connoisseurs, isn't it just a shade vulgar?*'

I coughed a fleck of blood from my left lung yesterday. But it was only one fleck; and that isn't serious. There's nothing basically wrong with my bellows. I blame the cold more than anything: it sticks daggers in a fellow's chest . . .

Twenty-three

MIKHAIL WOKE WITH a hangover. It didn't take the form of a headache, so much as of a certain sweatiness coupled with a strong desire to remain horizontal.

A table lamp, silk shade baked brown by the years, had been left on as though he were a child, subject to bad dreams. He squinted at it. The bulb seemed preternaturally bright, as if it had been sneakily increasing its luminosity all night long. Uttering a faint groan, he groped for the switch—which was damned stiff, and set far too high up the neck of the lamp. Always a battle switching off one of these things! Usually it ended with the lamp lying on the floor, blazing away stubbornly.

A pair of vinegar-brown bloomers caught his attention. These, and an elasticated bra, were tangled up with his own black acetate shorts on the floor. On closer, bleary inspection he detected a heap of woollen chainmail lying underneath, beside his trousers.

Turning over, he found to his surprise that what was crushing his spine was not a displaced bolster, but Dr Sonya Suslova . . .

He propped himself stiffly on one arm. Unpeeling the sheet, he inspected her breasts. They lay sluggishly parchmented by sleep, the nipples softly dissolved so that they had almost sunken into pits.

Sonya woke and blinked. Hastily she pulled the sheet right up to her chin. "Oh!" she said, her blue eyes widening.

"Good morning! God, I feel I've been through a mangle . . . I guess we must have made love last night?" This was not, he realized, a very tactful way of juxtaposing his hangover, and her.

She yawned, granting him a vision of the pink cave of her mouth

119

and throat, uvula pressing against arched tongue like a large clitoris. Her mouth snapped shut. "Can't you remember?"

"Er . . . Afraid it's all a bit hazy. Well, did we?"

"It seems highly likely we did, since we're lying in bed together!" She giggled.

Mikhail leaned over her. "Perhaps we ought to jog our memories?"

However, Sonya popped out of bed, hauling the sheet around her. "What's the time?"

Mikhail saw his watch lying under the lamp. "Seven. Bit after." Automatically he scooped up the watch and began winding it.

What a dumb thing, to fuss on with a watch when there's a naked woman in the bedroom! But actually, the clockwork watch was a vital link with reality. A watch was the only means left to them to measure time, when darkness and daylight had both melted into the same amorphous pearly mist . . .

Rolling off the bed, naked, he stood up with an effort and made for the window. Parting the chintz curtains, he inspected the luminous fog; it looked just as empty of content as yesterday. By the time he turned away—and this wasn't long—Sonya somehow had managed to dress herself at top speed. Already she was buttoning up her calico blouse. Thus, from being a hopeful lover, he was transformed into a patient standing starkers in a surgery—so that the Doctor could diagnose knobbly knees, or something. Stubbornly he sat down, still naked, and crossed his legs. Something was nagging at him.

Restored to her chain-mail, Sonya grinned and perched on the bottom of the bed.

"That was what I call a party! All friends together, now. Even Sergey. Passed out on the sofa, he did—how theatrical!" She laughed, since she knew for a fact that all artists habitually drank themselves senseless, given half the chance, and succumbed in odd corners, careless of clothes and comfort. "Osip won't have much to say about it, either! Do you remember how he was dancing with Felix, singing those rude songs?"

120

"Vaguely." *What was nagging at him?*

A hazy memory emerged of Sonya clinging on for grim death to the banisters . . . Oh yes, they had been a Soviet mountaineering duo, and the stairs had been the Caucasus. They had crawled upstairs on their hands and knees—hence these bruises on his knees! This involved a good deal of giggly clutching to prevent either person from sliding into crevasses . . . And once they had scaled the cornice of the landing, he had spotted Osip weaving about below and given warning of the sighting of an *Almast*, the wild man of the mountains. Huddled on the floor together, they had peeped through the rails, terrified of falling down the precipice into his clutches . . . Camp Six, the Summit, had been his bedroom.

All this larking about seemed a long time ago. Much more recently than that, he'd . . . well, he'd been sound asleep.

And dreaming! The *K. E. Tsiolkovsky* had been falling through time, down towards Siberia! And Anton Pavlovich had been trekking relentlessly up the Angara River . . .

These things had happened while he lay in a drunken fugue in bed, with Sonya blotto beside him . . .

Suddenly events collapsed into the right order, and he trembled and clenched his teeth. He was possessed, and he knew he couldn't shake free—not by way of vodka, nor by fucking, nor even by sleep. The momentum of events was independent of him now, just as it was independent of Victor the Master Hypnotist.

"You should get dressed," Sonya said. "You're shivering."

"Not with cold, I ain't. Sonya, the whole thing's been ploughing on regardless! I remember now: after we fell asleep I was back in the time-ship—and I was up the Angara too. It wasn't any ordinary dream. Even when I'm unconscious, it's all carrying on. I can't stop it—none of us can. Are we all drugged? Is that it, Doctor Suslov? Is this an experiment to disorient people? Are technicians sitting in some basement underneath this building, listening in through microphones and smirking? Are *they* pumping out that filthy fog? What is it: clouds of mind-gas?"

"It certainly isn't *my* experiment! It isn't Victor's, either, or he wouldn't have got so drunk. No, of course it isn't an experiment!"

"What is it, then?"

"Time has come adrift. Because . . . because *it has*, that's what." Sonya looked torn between bursting into tears, and coming to mother him. "We're trapped in a time-bubble—like a soap-bubble. That's why we couldn't leave this place yesterday. We just walked around the inside of a bubble. Outside of the bubble it's . . . 1890, or 2090, I don't know."

"And this bubble will pop—when I reach Tunguska?"

"It has to, Mike. The world will spring back." She smiled wryly. "And meanwhile, we're still alive. You, in particular, we're very lively."

"Thanks for telling me!"

"You'd better get some clothes on—I'm *starving*." Sonya squirmed. "Actually I'll go and get washed first."

"Are we really alive, like other people?"

She made an uncertain gesture, and fled from his bedroom.

Twenty-four

OSIP, UNSHAVEN AND the worse for wear, nevertheless had managed to produce hot coffee, and ham and eggs, by what everyone agreed to call nine o'clock. He sat down at the dining table with the others. That cottony fog was still rubbing itself up against all the windows of the building—and he needed company. He dared not miss a word which might explain this crazy, supernatural situation.

Not that he was a secretly religious man—that sort of thing was all stuff and nonsense. Still, he wouldn't have minded having an icon about the place just at the moment. Purely for decoration.

He stared at the window every now and then, fearful that the fog might be seeping inside. If so, then you could walk upstairs—and find yourself back down at the bottom again! He shuffled his chair closer to Victor Kirilenko, seeking protection. 'Knowledge is Power', after all . . .

Kirilenko mopped fat off his plate with a slice of bread, thumped a slice of cheese down on top, and chewed.

"Um," he said. "Good thing we've got enough food to last a siege. Um, now Mike you're saying that this mental journey of yours just ploughs on at its own pace—whether we like it or not? Even if we hold no more sessions, it'll just continue?"

"Relentlessly. Like an avalanche."

"Um, interesting. I wonder—ah—suppose there really *is* a time-ship? And suppose your mind is strongly in key with it—so that this affects the present in a paranormal way. . ." Kirilenko waved his greasy crust at Mikhail. "Of course, there's one big discrepancy."

"What's that, then?" asked Osip.

Kirilenko explained patiently, "A discrepancy is an inconsistency—something which doesn't add up."

"I know that! I in't uneducated. I mean, what sort of discrep . . . discrep . . . *What is it?*"

"Ah. Well, the good ship *K. E. Tsiolkovsky* is supposed to crash in the Tunguska region in the year 1908, right? Thus accounting for the well documented and exactly dated enigma, with which we are all familiar. Yet Anton Chekhov is heading towards the same place in the year 1890—to investigate precisely the same event, which occurred in 1888! There's your discrepancy: twenty years of it."

"But how can the same thing happen at two different times, Professor?"

"Right now I believe it is equally probable that the Tunguska event happens in 1908 *and* in 1888—it's undecided. So what is going to decide it? Why, the observers of this event—namely us! Specifically, Mike. Just as soon as Mike witnesses the *Tsiolkovsky* exploding in 1908, then all this phoney business back in 1890 will collapse. Poof! The fog will roll away, and you'll have your authentic Chekhov heading for Sakhalin, as originally occurred. This other trip will be a ghost event with no substance."

"That's way beyond me, Professor. What causes a ghost, of an event?"

"Aha, there we have it in a word—and that word is 'cause'! If a ship travels back through time—mark you, I don't say that any such thing really exists—then obviously this disrupts cause and effect. Perhaps the passage of the ship sets up a sort of wake, composed of ghost events? But consider: maybe such ghosts are swirling around us all the time—ghosts of unfulfilled possibilities? Our normal consciousness only lets us experience a single chain of cause and effect. But these are extraordinary circumstances we're in, now. Mike is experiencing possibilities, as though they're real events—and the *K. E. Tsiolkovsky* is a superb metaphor for what's going on in his head. And maybe that's all it is: a metaphor."

"How about the fog?" insisted Osip. "And none of us being able to leave?"

"Mike's mind must be very powerful," said Sonya; she flushed.

"Indeed, he must be some kind of medium, without realizing it. Obviously his case would repay—"

"No thanks," interrupted Mikhail with alacrity, "I've no desire to spend the next ten years locked in a lab."

"Nor I, dear boy—that's why I said 'would repay'."

"Nobody's gonna lock you up, Professor." Osip edged even closer, as a duckling to its dam. He refilled Kirilenko's coffee cup, nudging and jostling him officiously.

"Your duty, Mike, is to steer this ship of your mind to a safe . . . well, that's to say, to its destruction—in the year 1908. You must *observe* that event, so that it really happens. And then we'll all be free of this imprisoning mesmerism."

"Is he a mesmerist, too?"

"You've heard of the Indian rope trick, Osip? Well, it's said that the Indian yogi performs this so-called trick by means of mass suggestion. I think we may well have run across an even stranger case of mass suggestion, here!"

"Do you mean it's all clear out there?" asked Sergey. "What, we could walk off down the hill—if we could only see how?"

"I'm starting to suspect it." Kirilenko steepled his hands as if in prayer.

"And Osip could phone out—?"

"How about that voice I heard? I in't making it up, Professor!"

"Of course you aren't. Isn't it curious, though, that you only heard the voice after Mikhail Petrov had used the phone?"

"Ah—"

"Might I voice one small objection?" asked Mikhail sarcastically. "A minor point, but how come I'm suddenly a master of mass suggestion when I'm such a dud actor—I mean, let's be frank!—that I need a hypnotist to make me any good?"

Yet Kirilenko was unabashed. "That's because of super-ability, don't you see? Your own repressed talent is to persuade audiences.

It's an actor's business to convince the audience utterly. The yogi and the method actor have a lot in common, Mike—but the yogi goes a stage further. The yogi weaves a *perfect* illusion. He does so by using a superconscious communication channel. Beyond voice. Beyond body language. Incidentally, the object of the exercise *wasn't* to enhance your talent—but that's what seems to have happened."

Sergey nodded ruefully. "Speaking as a member of the audience, I'm convinced. Though I'll never know how the hell I got the Volga swung round in that space—!"

"The trouble is," said Mikhail, "I'm convinced too. Oughtn't a yogi to be aware of what he's up to? I sure ain't."

"But are we really an audience in the strict sense?" asked Kirilenko. "Aren't we all very much active participants? Fellow conspirators, almost?"

Felix thrust his chair back noisily. "It's a good thing we didn't decide to make a film about the young Lenin! Or we'd really be in the soup."

"In that case, you wouldn't have chosen Petrov for the part."

"Heaven knows what games a Lenin look-alike would have got up to in your hands!"

"Look," said Sonya, "if we're all supposed to be fellow conspirators, I suggest we avoid blaming any particular individual, hmm?"

Sergey thumped on the table, jarring cups and cutlery. "I'm going to speak freely—as an intimate friend, seeing as we all toasted each other so sincerely last night. Audience, participants: I don't care! All this talk, when we should be getting on with it! If Mike says it's all carrying on regardless, I'll believe him—he was telling the truth about outside. I want to know what's going on with Anton and Anton Astrov. One thing I can tell you is that time's moving much more slowly for Astrov than it is for Anton. With him it's minutes, compared with days."

"No it isn't," said Felix. "Astrov is living through years of time, speeded up."

126

Kirilenko dropped his napkin, and arose. "Sergey's quite right—about getting on with it."

"Can I come with you?" begged Osip.

"If you clear up, first."

Osip fairly scurried.

Twenty-five

"I'M AFRAID I did it too quickly," said Anna Aksakova. "Look, my over-ride programme won't lock in."

"Never mind, forget it." Anton gazed at that whisking bowl of a viewscreen, which by now was only showing a tiny portion of the Earth. "What's going on down there, Yuri?"

Valentin consulted his datalscope. "It's 1917. The Revolution." He laughed bitterly. "Now you see it, now you don't—we're back in Czarist times already."

"I suppose that makes us dangerous revolutionaries? Forerunners of the Great Explosion . . ."

"Eh?"

"The Revolution."

"Oh, that explosion." Yuri tapped the isocalendar. "Well, that shouldn't worry the Czar for long. I make it three minutes till Tunguska."

Anton switched on his chin-mike. "Commander Astrov to All Crew. We have failed. Our ship will be destroyed in approximately three minutes. This will happen too quickly for any of us to feel pain—or even to realize. There's nothing to fear." He felt his pet fly buzzing in the little box in his pocket as if trying to escape. "For your information, we will drop out of flux in the year 1908. We believe the ship may well explode over the Tunguska region of Central Siberia. If it's any consolation, we're all about to become part of a great mystery. Goodbye to you all."

He switched off. They sat and waited.

*

"Thirty seconds to go," said Yuri.

"The flux-field's holding steady," reported Anna.

Sasha gestured at the screens, ablaze with light. "Massive ionisation effects—we must be visible for hundreds of kilometres."

"The field's off!"

Briefly, on some screens, they saw a brown and green landscape streaked with clouds far below. Then the ship lurched hugely, swinging askew as the thin air tore at its irregular contours, pitching it along a new course.

Yuri cried out in agony as G-forces smashed him against his straps, snapping ribs. From somewhere else in the ship came distant screams. And Anna Aksakova's head lolled sideways at an impossible angle . . .

The gyrating *Tsiolkovsky* pitched in a new direction. The shafts of the sickle and the hammer, the blunt hammer head, all were raging with the abrasion of the atmosphere, trying to tear apart from each other. But the ship had no time to break up.

Anton struggled for words. "Sasha! I—"

He fell through time, dazed and sickened by a strobing mosaic of visions which overloaded any attempt to make sense of them all. Everything which had happened since 1908 seemed to be flashing through his brain in images, burning it out cell by cell . . .

Images of war, of burning cities under siege, mobs rioting, trials, of jets dropping sticks of bombs, of spacecraft blasting off, and of new cities rising. The faces of Lenin, Hitler, Gandhi, Mao, Gagarin, Einstein, Shostakovich, Berryman, Qiang-Xi raced towards him, and away. Images of past time and images of his own time whirlpooled around, dragging him down through the vortex.

He screamed.

Like chaff burning off from a heat-shield, fragmentary visions streamed out of the sun-bright depths of the vortex. Flashes of Hiroshima, Stalingrad, Freedom Moonbase, the Great Comet of 2070, the March on Mecca, the reconstruction of the Eiffel Tower, the deification of the paranormal infant Claudia Rapuchini and her assassination . . .

He continued screaming.

All these fragments *did* form part of a mosaic. The shattered pieces flew together and became a face. It was his own face, each of the cells of his skin and flesh a separate bit of history . . . The same high forehead, the humorous wrinkles fanning from the sides of the eyes, the dark tousled hair. The face cast a shadow behind it, like a deathmask moulded from inside the head . . .

"Oh, let me *die*!"

He did not die. The mosaic face broke up, and he fell down the funnel of visions again. The whirlpool began to ripple nauseatingly, distorting everything he saw. Waves arose; they rushed up the funnel towards him, tearing images apart and reforming them upside-down or inside-out—warping faces, altering events. For a moment his own body seemed to knot itself into a Klein bottle shape, then it snapped back again . . .

Abruptly he dropped through the bottom of the funnel. He was still sitting in his Commander's seat, staring at the swirling fog on the screen. "What—?"

"But I'm alive," said Anna in wonder, nearby.

"My chest," mumbled Yuri—and he breathed in cautiously. "It's okay, it isn't smashed . . ."

"We're still alive!" Sasha cried. "But how can we be? Look: we're still diving towards the Earth—we haven't hit it yet. God, surely we don't have to live through that again! And again and again and again!"

"Flux-field's back on," said Anna. "According to this it's never been off."

Yuri waved at the datalscope. "We're back in 1905. We missed Tunguska."

"But we didn't miss it—we exploded!"

"And still we're heading down the years."

"Towards what, *another* collision?"

"Around 1890. No, a bit earlier."

"Do we have to hit and hit and hit again—like a stone bouncing over a lake, before we can sink? I can't bear it, not again."

"This is your time-storm, Anna," Anton said. "This is what it's like."

Twenty-six

. . . AND AS SOON as Baron Nikolai Vershinin awakes from sleep
in the rude hut at Vanavara, he feels the warmth of the Countess's
naked body next to his, and rejoices that he has enjoyed such
ecstasy as on the previous night. Surely he can enjoy this same
ecstasy one more time before they get ready to be ferried over the
Stony Tunguska River into a savage landscape, where they will
have to sleep fully kitted out in fur coats and boots.

He pulls the bedding down a little way to contemplate the faint,
blurred outline of Lydia's face and shoulders in the grey of
dawn—in their haste they had left the window only partly
curtained.

The snow on the ledge and the leaves of frost on the panes focus,
as in a lens, the faint light coldly upon the bed; the rest of the room
is as black as inside a cupboard.

The night before, Lydia made love to Nikolai in a way that he
thinks of as sincere. There was no inane chatter, no babble of
meaningless vows, no 'poetry'. Instead, in each other's arms they
had both released a tension which had been pent up in their souls
and bodies for many weeks—the product of a void in both their
lives, which he for his part had filled up with bearish growls, and
she for hers with eccentric behaviour.

As is the case with essentially frigid people, who need to rub their
bodies together in abandon as the only way of setting them on fire,
their love-making was sensuous and lustful. They had snatched at
their joys almost desperately, he and she.

To awaken her, Nikolai kisses her shoulders.

He whispers, "Darling Lydia", yet there is little love or passion in his voice, for they both owe a desperate, selfish duty to themselves . . .

Her lips move underneath his lips. "Kolya," she murmurs. There's a harshness in the way she says his name; it resembles the stubborn grating of a pair of adjacent boulders in a river which is rushing ever onward past them in flood, towards some mysterious and distant destiny. And thus she opens her embrace to him . . .

She's still half asleep, and she remains so, as though what takes place now is only the continuation of a haunted dream—and this relieves her of any sense of connexion with the rest of the day.

Later, she sits up. Candlelight vies with the ice-light. Having pulled on her lace-decorated chemise, she brushes out her chestnut hair. Vershinin lights a cigar; it's the last one he has left.

"What encounters there are in our lives!" he exclaims. But then he paces about the room monotonously like a caged tiger, wearied suddenly by the length of time it takes her to get ready. 'Just imagine *this*, every morning!' he thinks to himself, feeling a strange blend of lust and boredom.

"I wonder how Masha and Nastya are getting on?" Lydia asks idly. "Nastya's the sly one, you know! She stares at a closed door as though she can see right through the wood—as if a sixth sense tells her everything. It's quite disconcerting! But she's too young to understand any of it . . . ."

'So if I became your husband,' thinks Vershinin, 'then Nastya would watch my door all the time—to make sure I wasn't slipping out to your boudoir, or even smoking in bed! Why should a child exercise such a damnable tyranny, unless that's the way you want it to be? Unless it's your excuse . . .

'You're glad to be free of a dull fool of a husband . . . so now you frustrate yourself, to keep your freedom! Oh, you cut a fine figure, Lydia, you really do—with your German camera and your cigarettes and your dashing ways. And really, all the time, you're a slave—to liberty! That's it.'

At first Nikolai is delighted by his perspicacity; but then the suspicion dawns on him that Lydia and the wayward governess

133

Olga Franzovna are in reality secret lovers . . . Thinking back, it seems to him that when he kissed Lydia awake, it was not his own diminutive, Kolya, which she murmured so demandingly in reply—but rather 'Olya', diminutive of Olga, the name of her dream.

Such a thing isn't totally beyond his comprehension. It isn't even beyond his sympathy, swear as he might at such perversions in the Mess; prescribe, as he might, a swift phallic cure for them . . .

Had Lydia and Olga sworn blood brotherhood (or sisterhood), nicking their wrists with sharp knives, blending their bloodstreams? What impulsive, impetuous creatures they both had seemed to him—surely they both nursed strong desires!

'What's got into me?' he wonders. 'Such slander, against a woman I've just slept with!'

He puzzles on and on, convinced that he has never thought so deeply as this morning. It's as though Lydia has lit a taper of speculation deep in him, which is flickering its light into dark corners . . .

On impulse he catches and raises her wrist, to stare at the white skin closely, seeking for the faint crack of a long-healed scar.

"What on Earth?"

"You ought to wear a fine golden wristwatch, Lydia. I'll buy you one, some day."

"Who needs to know the time? It's always either too late, or too early."

Nikolai guffaws. "Not for us, it wasn't."

"You embarrass me, Baron. Have you lost your respect for me so soon?"

"Not a bit of it! I'm crazy about you—that's the trouble. Ach, love! I think love's a pretty dodgy proposition. A fellow can fall in love with a sheep, if he's lonely enough."

"But a sheep can't fall in love with him."

"Or a woman could fall in love with a governess."

"Really?" Lydia purses her lips. "I wouldn't know."

"God fell in love with the world, Lydia. And He composed flowers and rivers, and birds and trees and clouds, to woo us. But in our responses we're just like sheep. Munch, munch—not 'alf bad, this patch of grass! Munch, munch—this clover's a bit of all right! That's what everyone's really like inside. Yet Cupid's blind, and love's an enchantment which stops us from seeing the truth. But the enchantment wears off after a while: two years, or three at the most. So where's the use? Before you even get going, you're condemned!"

"Lust," she answers, "is sometimes far more honest."

"That's a true word you've spoken. It's because of confusing lust with love that we all get into trouble. Only God knows love."

"Because He doesn't know lust . . ."

"I think love is something you feel for people in anguish. It's a form of sympathy—it hasn't anything to do with beauty." And suddenly Nikolai kneels by Lydia's side, and to his surprise he bursts into tears. "Forgive me, lady! Forgive me for not feeling love for you—because you're beautiful! I'll tell you what anguish is. Anguish is an 'impossible love', not one you can fulfil—if you follow my drift?"

"I believe you're reading my heart, *mon chéri*. If I'd known you could read hearts, I don't think I should have made love to you! Imagine a world where everyone can read everyone's heart at a glance—how awful." She speaks lightly, though really this is the levity of deep pain. "*Voyez*: no hidden secrets, no enchantments, no impossibilities . . . Consequently, no love—ever again. *Bien, le fin d'amour*."

However, by now her hair is fully brushed. And somebody walks past the frosted window, down the snowy Vanavara street, banging two pieces of metal together noisily; alarmed, a pack-horse whinnies . . .

135

Twenty-seven

The Middle of Nowhere (alias a Tungusi camp on the Chambé River)

My most dear Masha,
We've left the 'metropolis' of Vanavara far behind. Mind you, it was hard enough getting there in the first place. Without Tolya to guide us, I'm sure it would have taken us twice the time to cover the distance.

Our compass was little use; the latitude was already too high for accurate magnetic readings. The map we had brought from Krasnoyarsk was mostly wishful thinking—so Mirek began making his own map. But the terrain was vilely confusing: such a chaos of rugged gullies and steep hills, with creeks snaking everywhere—and the larger of these still unfrozen, so that we had to plodge through them, while the smaller rivulets were iced over and camouflaged with snow, providing excellent pitfalls for us and the horses . . .

Yes, Tolya proved invaluable. But as our mutual comprehension improved, he started to act oddly—particularly during our stay in Vanavara itself, which Tsiolkovsky and I devoted to questioning witnesses of the explosion two years ago.

Naturally, we had already asked Tolya about the strange event; but given his bastard Russian it was hard to say exactly what his answers were. Now that we were this much closer to the area of devastation, and now that he saw us actively pursuing our enquiries, our Tungusi friend became at once jittery—and almost cloyingly coquettish. It seemed to me as if, with our camera and our theodolite and other wonderful gear, we had become a sort of magic talisman of protection for the man—a safe conduct, or lucky charm—yet one whose efficacy might fail at any moment, bringing down a terrible nemesis upon his head.

As I say, while we were in Vanavara, Konstantin Eduardovich and I interviewed a number of the more reliable local farmers and traders. Faithfully we copied down their tales of fearful thunder-claps, and a pillar of light flaring into the sky, followed by an oven-hot wind fierce enough to knock a man off his feet and bring sods tumbling from the roofs—and a black mushrooming cloud.

Countess Lydia snapped photographs of some of our informants, but then she got bored and took herself off for a snowy gallop on borrowed horses with Vershinin—supposedly to try to pot a hare—and that left the two of us to get on with the job, helped or hampered as the case may be by Sidorov and Tolya. Tolya had insisted on tagging along, though he was acting weirdly—and Sidorov also seemed to have suffered a sudden fit of nervous instability. At each additional vindication of the stories he originally related on that fatal night in the inn, our Ilya ("At your service!") Alexandrovich would grin inanely in a way suggesting quite clearly to me that he was incapable of separating the wheat from the chaff in any scientific manner. Boiled turnip head, boiled brains—alas!

As we tramped back from an outlying farm, Tsiolkovsky fell behind with Tolya—and the two men fell into a kind of conversation, leaving me with my spaniel Sidorov; and I gained the impression, from a few paces ahead, that rapport had somehow been achieved between our Tungusi with his hamstrung Russian, and half-deaf Konstantin.

This was amply confirmed later on, in the 'inn'.

Lydia and Vershinin hadn't yet returned. Sidorov was staring at the notes we'd taken, as though they were the Holy Bible. Tolya had gone off somewhere—and Mirek was poring over his charts.

Tsiolkovsky leaned over Mirek's shoulder, and planted a finger on the map about one hundred versts north of Vanavara. "From what Tolya says, the spaceship must have exploded about *here*."

Masha, if you have any sort of map of this area, you'll see that the Tunguska flows westwards from Vanavara towards its confluence with the Chambé. Our original plan was to have some more rafts knocked together, and head downstream, then somehow to haul our rafts up the Chambé—infested with rapids though we had learned it to be—until we reached the Makirta River. On the map the Makirta is a very sinuous watercourse, though Mirek surmised that the map-maker might have put in all those loops and twists just to make the river look like a river. Tsiolkovsky's finger was indicating a spot some way beyond the headwaters of the Makirta.

"Is that what he says? So that's where the meteor crater'll be . . ."

Tsiolkovsky turned a deaf ear to Mirek's remark. He traced a line from Vanavara directly north through a blank on the map.

"And here's the Tungusi track that Tolya'll show us—as far as his family's tents on the upper Chambé. We can stay there overnight. After that, it's up to us."

"Hang on," said Mirek, "this is where he comes into his own. It's his territory—he can't chicken out just short of the finishing post. We'd better offer him some more roubles."

"But he's scared—that's what he was trying to tell me, only it's a bit more complicated than that . . ."

"Is that why he stayed down south all summer? Because he's afraid?"

"It's partly that . . ."

"He promised to guide us, damn it! 'As far as we need to go.'"

"I think he meant: as far as we *ought* to go."

"I get the impression," said I, "that while he's our guide, equally we're his escorts."

"That's it in a nutshell!" exclaimed Konstantin. "He has what you might call family problems . . . Ach, families!" And

Tsiolkovsky got quite steamed up about it. "Families have rights over you. They make demands. You can bind yourself in slavery because of a family. It doesn't matter how much you all love each other, and care for each other—it's still slavery. As far as I'm concerned, true freedom and joy comes from the mind. It comes from thoughts, free of hidebound conventions! A family can cripple you . . . ."

If I might digress here, Masha, and venture quite frankly upon a delicate topic, well, it's perfectly true in theory that a man needs a wife, and a woman needs a husband in our society. But in practice where would I ever find a wife as attentive and understanding and ever-helpful as yourself? And where could you find a suitor whom I could fully trust to take care of you as you deserve? A suitor may have lots of attractive qualities on the surface, but if you aren't blinded by emotional caprice or by foolish desperation—a fear that it's all getting too late—then you'll soon find this wrong, and that wrong. In a word, you'll make a big mistake if you're too impetuous.

(I suspect, Masha, that I'm *not* going to send these pages to you after all. Why should I confuse you unnecessarily, when you're obviously perfectly happy with things as they are? As is your devoted brother . . .)

I could understand why Tsiolkovsky was all het up about the subject of the family. I'd gathered during the course of several conversations that his father was a bold and honest man—outspoken on politics and religion—and consequently he was a complete failure in life. (It's the rogues who thrive!) Tsiolkovsky's father was dismissed from his post as a forest ranger, which destroyed whatever home security the family had—and Konstantin had to rely on the home, since he couldn't easily make friends outside because of his deafness and gawkiness. Then to cap it all, his mother died when he was just thirteen. His father tried to be an inventor, but of course he got no thanks from the world for that—though he encouraged his son splendidly, all be it with precious few roubles in the purse. He remembers best from his childhood the thrill when his Mother presented him with a toy hydrogen balloon . . .

Compared with him, *we* enjoyed a real family life, eh Masha? No matter that it was presided over by a blundering, narrow-minded tyrant! (I suppose you remember how cleverly our mean and bigoted father dealt with the matter of that dead rat drowned in the barrel of oil—by calling in a priest to exorcise the ratty influence, so that by the next day the news was all over Taganrog, and nobody would stop by our grocery store for weeks?) We were a resilient lot—we needed to be—and even so it took its toll. All the more reason, I submit, for keeping our surviving family as closely together as possible! Anyway, I'm straying far from the point . . .

"What sort of family problems has our tribesman got?" asked Mirek.

"Well, it's all because of the spaceship exploding—"

"Ah yes, the meteorite. Did it hurt his family? Kill somebody?"

"Not exactly . . ."

"So it's the sickness among the reindeer—the herds dying off?"

"No! It's all because of an ignorant, superstitious reason! Tolya's grandfather was some kind of tribal sorcerer. The Tungusi aren't even Christians, you know."

"Are you? Am I?"

"What I mean is, they haven't even got to the stage where they can *reject* Christianity. Tolya's grandfather died just before the explosion, then the explosion itself scared them out of their wits—so the Tungusi all want Tolya to take over as witch-doctor, because he showed the right signs when he was a boy. He had fits or something, and frothed at the mouth and babbled. And he went through some kind of ordeal, which is secret. But he doesn't want to be the village sorcerer now. He's seen trading posts, he's learned a bit of Russian . . ."

No wonder there had been a few moments of rapport between these two men, superficially so different in their background and beliefs. Konstantin's feeble and lonely childhood had turned him into a genuine scientist—and Tolya's boyish fits and foaming at the mouth had thrust him into a similar role within *his* society; but Tolya's was a society which lacked any notion of science or reason. Had I even hinted at such a comparison, I suspect that Tsiolkovsky would have felt deeply insulted . . .

"What's wrong with Tolya's father?" asked Mirek. "Didn't he froth at the mouth enough to inherit the mantle from his dad?"

"No, you see their custom is for the sorcerer's son to provide for his father—then the grandson takes over, and *his* son provides for him . . ."

"So Tolya would have to get married quickly?"

"I think he was trying to escape his fate by staying on in Kezhma."

"Are the women as ugly as that?"

"I mean the fate of being witch-doctor. He doesn't want it."

"So why's he going back to it?"

"He really has no choice—those are his people. We Russians aren't, and he knows it now."

Now I understood in what way we were a talisman for Tolya. "We're a little bit of Russia going back home with him—a bit of the civilization he wants, and can't get to grips with: that's it, isn't it? The poor confused lad."

"I don't care, as long as he guides us!" said Mirek.

"We all have problems," Konstantin said. "It's a question of rising above them."

Oh yes indeed: rising above them on a toy hydrogen balloon— or in a 'jet-propelled' rocket ship . . .

So now, dear Masha, after another strenuous and freezing trek, we find ourselves in a genuine Tungusi tent on the south bank of the Chambé, accepting hospitality overnight before pressing on into the unknown—with or without our guide. Tolya, the long-lost prodigal, is back in the bosom of his people; and in this setting he seems a different breed of fellow from the one who accompanied us hither. He's in his proper place at last. And this place possesses

141

him—just as *I* would be possessed by a little country farm with a few fruit trees and a decent angling stream . . .

The Tungusi camp is passably habitable, if you're a savage. Which is another way of saying that life is no more degraded here, than your average Great Russian village. Instead of houses made of mud and wood, there are in this clearing half a dozen large conical tents sewn from reindeer hide. Instead of a church, there is . . . well, the mighty forest, I suppose.

These Asiatic herdsmen are amiable enough—because we have brought their lost son home; though we cannot exchange a single word with any of them, except through Tolya. But they have set a whole tent aside for our party, and they have feasted us royally on fish soup; and now it's time to sleep.

Goodnight, dear Masha.

Twenty-eight

"IT FIGURES!"

Kirilenko asked Sergey, "How do you mean?"

"Isn't it obvious? No sooner have you dubbed Mikhail a 'medium', than that Tolya fellow turns out to be a Siberian shaman—how about that, eh? Suggestible isn't the word for it."

"Please," asked Osip, "what's a shaman?"

"It's a magician," Sonya explained. "In a primitive tribe like the Evenki: the Tungusi, as they used to be called. Of course there aren't any shamans nowadays. But back in 1890 there would have been—it isn't implausible at all."

Osip squinted. "Maybe . . . it's a case of 'Set a thief to catch a thief'?"

"What do you mean by that?" There was a note of derision in Sergey's voice.

"Well, if Professor Kirilenko says Mr Petrov's a medium, and if that guide bloke back in 1890 is one of them an' all—if that's what you mean by 'magician', Miss . . ."

"Bravo, Osip! You amaze me." Kirilenko looked genuinely pleased. "'Set a thief to catch a thief', eh? A medium will be drawn to another medium . . . A good piece of reasoning. Ah, but there's a snag. Mike's supposed to be identifying himself with Chekhov, not with Tolya."

"I'd say he's identifying himself with every damn character in his head," Sergey said. "Why not one more? Let's really crowd the stage! Joe Stalin was exiled to Krasnoyarsk, wasn't he? When would that have been?"

143

"Later on," Felix said. "Stalin was born in 1879."

"So what's wrong with that? Makes him twenty-one in the year in question. Young firebrand like him: spent half his youth escaping from one place or another. Come on, Mike: let's have the man of steel fleeing through the forest, and bumping into our brave band. Tolya can tell his fortune."

"I told you, I don't have any *control* over this."

"Excuse me," said Osip, "but in my opinion we ought to leave Joseph Stalin right out of it."

"Very wise," agreed Felix. "That's irresponsible talk, Sergey."

"Very sorry, I'm sure."

"Anyway," went on Osip, "if we could stick to brass tacks for a minute, we're all in a bit of a fix, in't we? There's some kind of mass suggestion going on, right? What you might call a collective mesmerism? Like in a theatre, with a hypnotist up on a stage. Only, this time the hypnotist has fooled the whole audience, not just one dupe up front. What's more, he's hypnotised his self into the bargain. No one's in charge any longer—and there's no way out of the theatre, either. Nobody can see the exits."

"Perhaps you'd like to be the usher?"

"Somebody's got to be, but it in't me, Mr Gorodsky." Osip rubbed his bristly chin. "I'm just saying, who's going to clap their hands and cry, 'Wake up!'?"

"But we don't want to 'wake up' yet," said Kirilenko. "It's too soon. The expedition hasn't reached its goal, and the ship hasn't exploded. Well, in a manner of speaking it *has* exploded—"

"Only it's back in one piece again. Unfortunately," said Felix. "For us, and for all on board, and for Anton Chekhov, and for my great-aunt Anastasia. *Do* make a better go of it next time, Mike! Any clever American headshrinker could tell you that a spaceship is a great big phallic symbol. This failure to explode could do awful things to your love life—right, Dr Suslova?"

Sonya blushed. "Freudianism is a—"

144

"Jewish bourgeois mystification, eh?" Felix chuckled.

"More to the point," snapped Sonya, "the *K. E. Tsiolkovsky* doesn't remotely resemble a phallus."

"How do I know what Mikhail's dong looks like?"

Twenty-nine

A JINGLING OF metal woke Anton. This, and the sound of his name being called in a strange, faraway voice. But then he realized that the summons came from quite close by, only it seemed pitched for his ears alone.

A shimmering ghost stood in the open flap of the tent. Bright moonlight on the snow illuminated it. Anton grunted in alarm at the sight, producing a noise in his throat which sounded foreign to him, more like the cry or cough of some doomed animal far away.

"Antosha," the ghost called. "Come along with me."

Within the tent a single candle was still burning, though it was almost down to the stub. None of Anton's companions stirred in their sleep. Hastily he fumbled for the tin containing his pince-nez and slipped the glasses on.

Now that he could see clearly, what confronted him was even more disconcerting than a ghost might have been. The face of the apparition was that of a metal bird, with sharp iron beak and cheek-feathers of rusty iron. Its eyes were dark holes. On its head the creature wore a felt cap with kopecks sewn around it. A caftan hung from its shoulders, decked with long ribbons upon which were sewn dozens of pieces of metal shaped into suns and moons and stars. When the figure shifted, these ribbons swayed like snakes, all the pieces jangling together. What a firmament of stars and discs! What a weight they must be! Nor was that the whole of the metal: an iron breastplate was fastened to the creature's chest with rope . . .

In one hand the visitor held a little drum; and in the other a wooden staff—the head of the staff was carved into a horse head.

And none of the other sleepers woke . . . Obviously the monster must be one of the Tungusi, dressed up in the middle of the night like a pagan Archimandrite. Why? To kill them and rob them? Nobody would ever find out. There would be no justice—only murder. Anton's thoughts raced fearfully. *'Where the hell's that revolver?'*

"Jaroslav, wake up!" He gripped Mirek by the shoulder and shook him; but the Czech only grunted and slumbered on.

"He won't wake," said the visitor. "None will. Only you. I only called you."

"Tolya, is that you? But you're speaking Russian—quite passably!"

"A man understands all tongues when he speaks the tongue of Nature."

"Really? *Alors, parlez avec moi en français!*"

"Russian's good enough."

"You *are* Tolya—that's your voice."

"I am Shaman."

"Who?"

"You don't speak Tungus'k. Never mind. Give me some tobacco and come outside."

"So you want me to hand over my tobacco!"

"Just a mouthful, no more. I need tobacco to chew. You give it—it has to be your tobacco."

"But what for?"

"To let me dream."

Reluctantly Anton searched his bag in the candlelight for his precious stock of decent Ukrainian weed, mailed by Masha. Tolya—who else would it be?—trotted over. Depositing staff and drum briefly, he scooped up a handful of tobacco. Raising the metal bird-mask a little, he crammed the spoils between his lips and began noisily masticating them. Then he beat a hasty retreat back to the tent flap, and held it wide. "Come!"

Non-plussed, Anton donned his boots, hugged his clothes about him, and followed.

Tolya skipped away smartly into the centre of the clearing and began dancing slowly round and round—but with the light step of a ballet dancer, not like someone encumbered with such a weight of metal. The iron stars clashed and sparkled in the moonlight, but in spite of the clanking of all these medallions nobody peeped out of any of the tents. Even the hobbled horses stood like statues. A trance had fallen upon the world, beyond the trance of sleep.

The great pines and larches that hemmed the clearing were frost-giants crowding together to watch. Anton could just see the river beyond, in one direction. Little ice floes raced along it, spinning and colliding.

'Dream people will slip out of the trees soon,' he thought to himself. 'And out of the past they'll slip, too—grinning and sneering, their hearts full of intrigue. Then I'll look around, and Masha will be there and everybody else I love, all of them suffering stupid cruelties at the hands of my bogies . . .'

However, nobody came from the world of memory; and Tolya spun himself to a standstill. Flopping cross-legged on to the snow, his metalled ribbons spreading round him in a tiny tent, he began to rap his drum with a stick pulled from inside his caftan.

Rut-tut-tut! Rut-tut-tut! Rit-tit-tit!

Then he tossed his drumstick into the air. It turned over and over, and fell at Anton's feet, where it jerked about for a moment like a compass needle before coming to rest, pointing north by south.

"Heat!" moaned the strange figure. "Unbearable heat! The heat of Ogdy burning all the trees which are the roadway from Earth to Sky. But Shaman don't feel no heat!"

Tolya jumped up again suddenly, as if his tail was on fire. Racing towards the closest of the towering, snow-draped firs, he ducked underneath the bottom branches, then heedless of all the pounds of metal he was wearing, he leaped, caught hold, and scrambled up the trunk from branch to branch—showering snow down—till he sat perched on a high limb.

Staring up at the brittle, ice-flake stars in the sky, he cried,

"Lord Buga! Here I am, back where I was before my birth! Before the time my soul got hauled down from the branches of the World Tree—oh, Tree of all the World! D'you hear me?"

Amazed, Anton walked forward a few paces.

"Lord Buga, all your trees lie flat! What does it mean? Has Ogdy won out over you? Has He thrown down the sky-ladder? Must we all decay into beasts of no wisdom?"

The iron bird cocked its head, listening. Then it shinned down the tree trunk again, and ducked out into the clearing to stand rocking and jingling before Anton. Somewhere inside the dark holes of its mask, glassy eyes stared into his own eyes. Tolya tipped the mask up momentarily, just a little, and spat a brown spent wad into the snow.

Confronted by this tribal gibberer—who was undeniably impressive in an eerie, primitive way in the haunted moonlight—Anton felt as if time had been dislocated, and he had been suddenly plunged a thousand years into the past. Here was the real World Soul that Lydia had invoked so lyrically and fatuously as they floated down the Yenisey!

Superstition . . . and absurd ecstasies . . . and weary despair—and sheer terror of some malicious spiritual foe lurking in the vastness of the land: these were all the common currency of average Christian souls, at the best of times! Was Tolya really any different from them—or they from him? There was a suspicious similarity between Tolya's 'Lord Buga' and the Russian word for God . . .

"I hear you!" the figure cried. It performed antic capers. "He shall see! And only he! Then he will turn his steps away from the accursed place!"

Tolya whipped out an oval mirror from inside his caftan. It was the size of his palm, and framed in bronze. Puffing, he polished with his cuff before his breath could freeze.

"Antosha, look!"

And Anton looked. To begin with, it appeared that the silvering behind the glass was badly tarnished; he could only make out a

149

snowstorm or white fog, in place of the clearing . . . But then the fog (or whatever) dispersed suddenly. To his surprise he saw what must be the bridge of a ship, in miniature within. At least so he assumed from all the glass dials, instruments and controls. As the mirror tipped slightly in Tolya's hand, he could see a man strapped in a seat. The man wore a worried expression on his face—and that face, astonishingly, was *Anton's own.*

Who *was* the man?

He could hardly be a naval officer. He was wearing such a peculiar uniform: silver-grey, and all of a piece, with strips of metal on the pockets. A red flag was sewn to his sleeve, near the shoulder, sporting a star and a hammer and sickle. What kind of flag was that? Turkish? No . . .

As Anton watched, the other man who wore his face fumbled with the buckles holding him—and floated up above the seat. Weightlessly.

Was this not a ship at sea at all—but one of Tsiolkovsky's spaceships? But if there were people on Mars—where they must fly the red flag—why should they look exactly like people on Earth? Was a twin born on Mars, to every soul on Earth?

This had to be a hallucination—a person could be mesmerised by a mirror! Anton shook his head, to regain clarity; and in response Tolya shook the mirror from side to side . . .

Anton blinked. The scene had changed. His double was lying on a tatty old sofa in a wood-panelled room. A burly man with curly black hair and a thin nose, dressed in a suit of indefinably strange cut, was sitting astride a cane chair nearby—like a doctor by his patient's couch. The 'double' must have hurt his eye; he was wearing a black patch over it . . . His head rested on a folded jacket; otherwise he was dressed in a woollen jersey and a pair of coarse blue trousers apparently cut from sailcloth or tent canvas.

A peculiar box stood on the floor beside the sofa. It was the size of a small suitcase, and what appeared to be glass discs joined by a length of grey tape were turning round on top of it while the doctor listened intently to the words of the invalid . . . Since Anton couldn't lipread, whatever was being related remained a mystery—or why the doctor should be glancing at the box from time to time, as though this was his tool of diagnosis.

Suddenly Anton began to feel that he was falling forward weightlessly—and that in a very short while he would *be* that figure lying on the sofa! He cried out incoherently.

A jerk upon his wrist broke the enchantment. He discovered that Tolya had cast a little noose of twine around his wrist, with his free hand. The Tungusi was playing him as an angler plays a fish . . . And the mirror was all snow or fog again; quickly Tolya tucked it back inside his caftan out of sight.

"So you're back?" said Tolya. "Make sure you *go* back, where you belong."

"What did I see? What was it? Where was it?"

"You should rather ask: *When* was it?"

"When? What do you mean by that?"

The Tungusi chuckled softly, and led Anton unresistingly back towards the tent, pulling him along by that loop of string. And one of the horses neighed miserably: a statue restored to life . . .

Weariness overcame Anton the moment the two men reached the tent flap. He was barely able to pull his boots off in the last guttering flickers from the candle, and creep back inside his bedding, before he fell deeply asleep.

Thirty

NEXT MORNING TOLYA gave no sign that anything odd had happened between Anton and him the night before; what's more he talked in the same barbaric and halting Russian as ever. So Anton wasn't at all convinced that his nocturnal experience had been anything other than a particularly vivid dream. Perhaps he had walked in his sleep, in the clearing . . .

After a lot of grumbling on Tolya's part, considerable browbeating by Vershinin and a mite of bribery from Mirek, the Tungusi even agreed to guide them further towards their destination; and within a couple of hours the party was making its way along the south bank of the Chambé in an easterly direction. The day was bitterly cold, though hardly a breeze was stirring; and under a cloudless sky that augured well—though not to Tolya— the snow was almost blue, not white. So low must the temperature have been that the snow ran off their boots and the horses' hooves and the sledge-runners like dry dust; none of it could cling.

A couple of versts beyond the Tungusi encampment they reached the Avarkita and waded across it amidst little rafts of ice; after which they had to light a bonfire of branches and stamp around to dry their legs. Five versts further on Tolya pointed out the best place to cross the Chambé itself, then he took them to where a single raft was cached, hidden by snow amidst tall spruces.

He pointed north by north-west. "Before noon, see trees what fell down. I go now."

"Oh no you don't!" barked Vershinin. He caught hold of Tolya's arm. "You're coming along too! How are we supposed to

152

find the trail on our own? We're paying you good roubles—a lot more than you deserve!"

"Is cursed."

"Drivel! What's wrong with our money? Your eyes lit up before."

"Money clean. Place cursed."

"Balderdash and poppycock!"

"I don't know about that," said Tsiolkovsky thoughtfully. "It occurs to me that if billions of atoms get broken, and if these fragments impregnate the ground, then conceivably the earth continues to release active particles—"

"Shut up." Vershinin pulled out his service revolver and waved it about.

"Let's try to be rational?" suggested Mirek.

"What's rational about a curse? I ask you! Tell me, my northern savage, how can any part of God's good Earth be cursed? This might be a wretched, desolate hole, and the conditions of life might be shit, but *cursed*—isn't that going a bit far?" He rounded on Mirek for a moment. "Are you going to let us all be stymied by a curse? I'll tell you what kind of curses I believe in! Curses that get things done!"

"Quite so," said Lydia. "But *do* put the gun away."

"You not see," Tolya said. "Is curse."

As Vershinin was holstering his revolver, obedient to her word, Tsiolkovsky began mumbling. "Such particles . . . they might well involve, um, a form of *burning* energy . . . like the sun's energy . . ."

"Be quiet, drudge! Come along, wild man, tell us all about this precious curse! What does it do? Make people's balls fall off?"

"It belong Tungusi people."

"Aha!" There was a glint in Mirek's eye. "Do I hear someone invoking mineral rights? One has to realise that even *if* mining is possible, this will require tens of thousands of roubles in investment capital before utilisation—"

"He means," interrupted Anton, "that Ogdy—their god of fire,

153

or of heat and cold or something—has dethroned their sky god, Buga, by knocking down all the trees."

"How on Earth do you know that?" Sidorov's expression was a study in doting wonder. On Tolya's face, however, was a different expression: one of complete surprise at this revelation—as though he hadn't said it all in Anton's hearing just a few hours earlier . . .

'And maybe he never did,' thought Anton. 'Not if I was dreaming . . . But what if Tolya was in some sort of trance last night? A trance in which he spoke much better Russian than he normally does? His brain soaks up the Russian language like a sponge, but only the top of the sponge is ever in touch with the surface—last night he spoke from the depths.'

Sensing that somehow he had gained the upper hand, Anton fixed Tolya with what he hoped was a look of penetrating command. "You *will* guide us—all the way."

The Tungusi glanced aside, like a village dog, outstared. Presently he nodded.

'Maybe,' Anton reflected, 'all that nonsense last night was supposed to send me scuttling with my tail between my legs . . . on the principle that it would have sent a Tungusi scuttling!'

He turned to Vershinin, and spoke angrily. "They may be wild men! And what this place needs *are* mines and railways and dispensaries and schools! But how can we even think of this when Russia herself is so uncivilised? When pig ignorance rules the roost everywhere? I tell you, Baron, it's the ordinary Russian people who are devils of ignorance—not just these tribesmen!"

He found himself remembering the red flag stitched to the clothes of his double in the mirror . . . A hammer and sickle—all the way from the Red Planet. Symbols of hard work which had successfully built a ship of space? Yes, that's what they might have been: emblems of honest, clear-sighted labour.

"And what's more," he said to Mirek, "our local socialists aren't likely to change things much! What do they call themselves: Marxists, eh? Lackeys of a German Jew's dogmas . . . All they can produce are tiny explosions of mayhem which only make matters worse. If society's ever going to change, maybe the impetus will *have* to come from the planet Mars!"

The immediate effect of Anton's outburst, in the dry chill air, was to rack him with a bronchial spasm. He coughed into his glove eight or ten times. Exhausted, he continued staring at his gloved fist. On the fabric he saw a tiny red star, of bloody sputum.

By late afternoon they had been struggling through devastation for many versts. Uncountable pines and birches had been blasted to the ground. Under the snow cover the taiga seemed to be an infinite battlefield where massed armies of giants had been laid low, doomed to lie here for several hundred years till very slowly they rotted away, summer by summer. All the tumbled trunks pointed south.

Yet branches and wrenched-up roots twisted every which way, too, like bare broken bones—the force of the blast had instantly stripped away all trace of former greenery from the branches. So the only way though very often was to hack a path with axe or sickle.

But they made progress.

To the east the land sloped downward, and there they could see the River Makirta approaching them and twisting away again a dozen times over; at least the map was right in that respect. Low knolls pimpled the terrain. Lydia had scrambled up several of these with Mirek, she to gain a little elevation for photography, he to take sightings through his theodolite.

In worsening weather late in the day, they camped. A bitter wind was blowing steadily from the west by now, raking their cheeks; it seemed to be scudding grits of ice into their skin instead of snowflakes. If the wind had been coming from the north, it would hardly have been possible to breathe.

A couple of hours earlier they had all rubbed their faces with goose grease. It had been Mirek's inspiration to bring along jars of this thick sticky fat: a piece of forethought for which Lydia thanked him profusely while she rescued her complexion from

155

ruin. Anton, who had been trudging in a daze, thought for a while that they were all donning theatrical grease paint, a commodity from another world—to which he doubted if he would ever again belong . . . He feared he was going to lose the sight of his weaker eye. He had wept tears from it, and these tears froze on his cheek, notwithstanding the grease. These tears of ice only melted after quite a while inside the chilly tent which they erected finally in the lee of a knoll.

He and Sidorov, Mirek, Tolya and Tsiolkovsky all crammed into a single tent, huddling for warmth which seemed to elude them. Lydia and Vershinin shared a second, smaller tent pitched close by; though there was no doubt in Anton's mind as to their . . . frigidity, in the circumstances. It was enough agony to expose yourself momentarily outside for a piss, with your back to the wind; and the yellow stain on the snow froze instantly. As for having a crap the following morning, he certainly intended to hold *that* back for as long as possible, till it was all ready to burst out in one five-second rush. No, Lydia and Kolya weren't making love . . .

Anton drifted slowly off to sleep, fully dressed, as though succumbing to exposure.

He was lost in a great house made all of ice . . . Desperately he tried to find the room where sister Masha and mother Evgenia were praying for him—the room with the icon. He wanted so much to light a candle in memory of his father.

But these ice walls were as reflective as mirrors; so that he kept on turning corners and bumping into himself. These sudden contacts with his own image chilled him to the marrow.

Eventually his image spoke to him.

"Hullo there," it said in a chirpy way. "My name's Mike. I'm an actor—star of provincial stage and screen!" (What sort of screen could he possibly mean?) "I'm acting *you*, old Antosha. And *you're* acting *me* . . ."

The image faded. The ice wall ran with moisture as though weeping. Through the halls of ice Anton heard Tolya's mocking laughter echo. At once he awoke, sweating and shivering—the sweat seeming to freeze as soon as it oozed out of him. His arm had thrashed about and fallen across Tolya's body. Bitterly Anton turned over to face the other way.

Thirty-one

"TIME-STORM? IT'S JUST a word I made up—an empty noise!"

"Even so, Anna."

"Well, supposing this *is* a time-storm—whatever such a thing might be. What does that tell us? Nothing at all! We're none the wiser."

"Yuri, did we pick up any temporal momentum there?"

"Uh . . . Yes, you're right! We picked up almost 20 chronodynes. That isn't as much as we lost to the American Shield."

"No, it wouldn't be. Listen," said Anton. "the temporal momentum we lost to the Shield must have been discharging itself back through history from our starting point. Try to imagine it as a tidal wave running the wrong way up a river—and gradually losing power. I think the wave caught up with us just now—in 1908. It discharged its remaining momentum, and boosted our flux-field. Result: it tossed us back *beyond* 1908."

"But we all *died*! I'm sure I died," said Anna Aksakova.

"Oh, we did die—make no mistake. But then history altered; and we hadn't died, after all. What happens now is that we're going to explode in 1888."

"But this is mad! What about Tunguska in 1908?"

"Nothing will happen in 1908, Anna—not now. For a while it was reality, then the storm overtook us. The wave caught up. It thrust us further back."

"Are you saying we've changed history?" asked Sasha indignantly.

"Maybe there are a million streams of time? Each one with its own unique history? Some similar, some wildly different. A wave

158

built up behind us, surging against the current. It was a wave of our own causing. Yes, I see it now! The wave burst the banks, and washed us into a different stream—so it could dissipate its energy. Now the streams are settling down again. Soon everything will be flowing the right way. Just as soon as we hit the 1880s."

Yuri cackled. "What does it matter when we explode? Nobody paid much attention in 1908. You can bet on even less attention in the 1880s."

"So we won't kill anybody's grandmother," Anton said. "Hitler and Stalin will still be born. The October Revolution will happen on time. And *we'll* all be born, too, in time—and we'll fly backwards through time."

"*We* will?" Sasha struggled to express herself. "But *we* know that Tunguska happened in 1908!"

With an effort Yuri Valentin pulled himself together. "Maybe you're right about there being more than one stream of time," he said to Anton. "But I don't see how there can be millions of streams, like you just said. Maybe there are just two—with one main difference between them: the date when we crash. And that's because . . . it's *us* who split time. So in this present stream the wave catches up with us and bounces us back to 1888, cancelling Tunguska-1908. Time rolls by. We all grow up in a Tunguska-1888 framework —and that won't make a scrap of difference to the world! The *Tsiolkovsky* sets off again, and the same thing goes wrong—but this time we're heading for a crash in '88. Just as we explode, the wave catches up—and bounces us forward into a 1908 framework. Which doesn't make a scrap of difference to the world . . ."

"So we set off again?" said Anna. "And travel round the same loop for ever and ever? I can't bear it." She began to gasp for breath, as though she wanted to weep but was empty inside.

Yuri tried to reassure her. "It won't affect us like that, Anna. We die once, then twice—and that's the end of it, I'm sure."

"But these two streams *must* alternate," said Sasha. "For ever and for ever. Over and over again. Or else the pattern wouldn't work. The streams are mutual—they're braided together. Your

1888-explosion world has to be followed by a 1908-explosion world. That one has to be followed by an 1888-world. Ad infinitum."

"Yes, but don't you see, these two possible sequences will always be exactly the same, no matter how often each is repeated? They'll each of them be identical in themselves. It's impossible to distinguish between identical events that occupy the same patch of space-time—so we can't be conscious of any repetition. Look, our successors—that's the best way to think of them—our successors will live out their 1888-framework lives, and they'll die in 1908. Then *their* successors, who'll be identical to us, will live out their *own* lives—and they'll be *us*. I'll be saying exactly what I'm saying now. It *will* be me. It *is*, present tense. They aren't really our successors—they're us."

Anton had been fiddling with his moustache. He chuckled. "Okay, this can't be the first time round, can it? It must be happening an infinite number of identical times—and it's never caused me grief before! You could even say we've become immortal, in a funny sort of way. Not that I ever noticed it before . . . Well done, Yuri, lad. What year is it, by the way?"

"1895. You aren't surely going to tell the crew, *again*?"

"Doubt if I could explain in time! If they're immortal, they're immortal. And right now they must think they've been reprieved. It's like Dostoevsky in front of the firing squad. It would be too cruel to set them up again. Anyway . . ." He hesitated.

"Anyway," said Sasha—and she was shivering, with goose bumps on her skin, "we've no guarantee that we'll die, and an end of it, this time *either*. Maybe there's a closed loop between 1908 and 1888. Maybe this *is* the first time, and we just bounce back and forth from now on, altering reality and altering it back again— because the Cosmic Censorship won't allow reality to be altered. Maybe we'll die and die and die forever!"

Anton leaned over to dig her in the ribs. "Look on the bright side, darling! We'd really be immortal then, and know all about it. So we'd get very very wise—apart from the slight distraction of being killed every ten minutes or so. They say you can get used to anything."

"No, it can't be that way," said Yuri. "The whole of history from the 1880s on has to be involved. I'll tell you why: just before I died I saw images of events and personalities streaming past me."

"Ah, you as well?"

"Those images were from the whole period right up to our own day. That's how far the braid extends."

"I saw that too," said Sasha. "And I saw a face, as well—just at the very end, before I found myself alive again."

"Yes, the face," agreed Yuri. "I saw the face."

"I didn't," said Anna sharply. "I didn't see any history either!"

"That's because you broke your neck *before* we exploded," said Anton. "Can't expect to see things when you break your neck. So you saw your own face, Yuri, did you?"

"No! Of course not. I saw yours."

"So did I," said Sasha. "But it wasn't quite your face—there was something different about it, as if it was your twin brother's face."

"Only, I don't have a twin brother . . . Or do I? Maybe that was Anton Astrov, Mark 2, in the Tunguska-'88 framework—waiting in the wings?"

Ionisation effects suddenly enflamed all the viewscreens, like jets of gas in burning ovens . . .

"And there was another face behind that face. It was wearing old-fashioned spectacles—what did they call them?" Sasha mimed.

"Pince-nez," said Yuri. "That's right: there was one face wearing another face that was almost the same!"

"Flux-field off!" This time Anna hunched, to protect her neck . . .

Thirty-two

BY NOON NEXT day they had crossed the headwaters of the Makirta only fifteen or so versts from its source. Here the stream was shallow enough to ford without a soaking, though the waters were still sufficiently angry to stop ice from crusting them over. The bitter wind of yesterday had slackened to a chilly breeze.

As they toiled up the slope of Khladni Ridge six versts beyond the Makirta, hacking a path through the snow-thatched tangle of tree bones, it became evident that the upper heights of the felled larches had not simply been stripped bare—they had been scorched into the bargain.

Not even a cosmetic covering of snow could conceal this fact. The fist of wind which had felled these giants had been intensely hot. It might well have come from a limb of the sun itself. Many of the trees looked as though their tops had been thrust into a white-hot furnace.

Yet strangely, in the aftermath of this incandescent blow, no forest fire had raged across the wrecked taiga; otherwise all the fallen timber would have been reduced to ash. Maybe the very air had been torn away from the ruined forest, suffocating the flames even as they were lit . . .

A few times they stopped to sweep snow free from the corpses of these trees so that Lydia could photograph the charring of the wood. Tsiolkovsky would fumble with a pencil in his glove, scribbling hasty calculations of units of heat and energy.

At the top of Khladni Ridge the party halted, in awe at the view from this high point.

They could see tens of versts northward over the hilly terrain, as far as the snow-shrouded hills along the distant Khushmo River. And all across this huge expanse everything had been burned and blasted to the ground. Eastwards, far away in the lee of some craggy hills, a few patches of forest still survived intact where they had been sheltered from the shockwave. In the ultimate distance right on the eastern horizon they could make out where the living taiga resumed its march across the land . . .

With theodolite and binoculars, Mirek and Vershinin took the measure of this terrain of hell; while Lydia used up two whole rolls of her German film.

Presently Ilya Sidorov fell to his knees in the snow as if to pray. He was overwhelmed. "Oh God," he wailed. "We're such insignificant creatures! What can a human being ever hope to achieve—in view of this?"

"Get a grip on yourself!" growled Vershinin. "Damn it, you ought to be feeling vindicated. Here it is, and it's all true."

Tolya regarded the stooped man with glee. "Place cursed. So is you."

"Shut your face!" shouted the Baron.

Mirek glanced round from his theodolite. "Do you realize, we aren't even *near* the centre yet?" He pointed. "See how all the trees are still lying pretty well parallel, pointing back the way we came? The meteorite must have struck the ground at least another twenty versts north of here. That's why we can't see any crater. When we do, it'll be enormous! The Arizona one won't be a patch on it. Frankly, I'm surprised the ground isn't riven into fissures and strewn with fallen boulders even this far away."

Tsiolkovsky banged his hands together to restore his life-blood to them. "That's because the spaceship exploded in the sky." He gestured upwards, "It must have become a little sun for a few seconds. Imagine the power locked in it! Actually, there's no need to imagine—it can all be calculated."

"Power?" Sidorov parroted the word. "We're powerless, and no denying it . . ."

163

Tsiolkovsky moved over to comfort him. "Ilya Alexandrovich, we too will learn to unlock the power of the sun!"

Vershinin, the professional soldier, eyed the scientist thoughtfully. "Is that wise? Just look over there: suppose this was Moscow, and your ship had been exploded over it by design—as a weapon. Why, there wouldn't be a building left standing. And as for people: noble and peasant, merchant and priest alike—all dead in a flash. I tell you, as a military man the very prospect appals me. Where's the point in valour or discipline in such circumstances? It would mean the end of war as a heroic activity. Your sort of people would be ruling the roost, not officers and nobles."

"Nobles, indeed!" Anton spoke bitterly. "When every noble spawns a dozen other nobles, sometimes nobility runs quite thin . . ."

"This is hardly the place for us to fight a duel, Anton Pavlovich! This is the aftermath of battle—waged between the Present and the Future. If Tsiolkovsky has his way, we'll all be the losers."

"Sorry, I wasn't trying to be offensive . . . In many respects I agree with you. I mean, it would be pointless for a chap to do anything for his country—if a Napoleon of the future can simply send one ship to explode over Moscow, and destroy it all in five seconds . . ."

Sidorov struggled to his feet. "A world without meaning . . . isn't the world absurd enough already?"

"Some of the fellows in it are!" snapped Vershinin. "Tell me something, Anton Pavlovich: supposing the world *did* become as absurd as this, how would you artist chappies go about ennobling the human race, then?"

It appeared to be a serious question, so Anton tried to answer it. "Possibly . . . artists would invent other worlds—where such things didn't happen? Possibly they'd even try to live entirely in those worlds, in their imaginations? I don't know, really . . . Maybe they might invent worlds which were even worse and more absurd—so that the real world seemed sane by contrast?"

Tsiolkovsky butted in. "Obviously the artists of the future will imagine other worlds! Worlds out in space—beyond the prison of the planet Earth! But you needn't worry about scientists destroying the world—they'll only use such power to liberate us."

Anton nodded. "Science is our best hope."

"True," said Vershinin. "It's just that I look at all this, and wonder . . ."

"Well, let's get on with some science!" said Mirek testily. "Take a look at those clouds—I'd say we're in for another spot of foul weather."

Tolya began to ramble. "Me, coward. Grandad could climb the sky. Now all knocked flat. Giants are dwarfs. You think it needs brave man to come here? Needs *creature*. Creature on string."

They ignored him.

Mirek was perfectly right about another turn in the weather. They encamped below Khladni Ridge that evening in a bitter blizzard, and the whole party crammed into a single tent. To leave the wretched horses exposed out in the open seemed the height of cruelty and insanity—the wind flayed you alive, the moment you set foot outside . . .

"Is anyone else alive in the whole world?" asked Lydia as they lay jumbled together in the darkness after eating, still too cold to sleep.

"It gets to you, doesn't it?" murmured Vershinin softly. "You have to be brave—you have to believe in yourself."

"Your photos will amaze people," Tsiolkovsky assured her. "They'll set the world on fire. So will my calculations, for that matter. This place will become a Mecca of science."

"Mecca, eh?" Anton sighed. "I once thought that Sakhalin ought to be a Russian Mecca—where people made pilgrimages for the good of their souls . . ."

Sidorov began to whine. "We'll probably all die out here—"

"We damn well won't!" thundered Vershinin. "You'll get back, you wretch, if I have to drag you personally."

165

But the wind howled its wolf-pack cry for their deaths, outside. It howled with huge, mindless indifference.

They weren't able to move during the whole of the next day. Even brief forays outside the tent to perform bodily functions or to try to tend to the horses, proved agonizing. Idiotically, they spent much of their time playing lotto for ten kopeck stakes.

"Eighty-one!" they called out; and "*Trente-quatre!*" and "Twenty-two!" Lotto wasn't really such a bad game, once you got used to it. Or perhaps their brains had simply frozen up . . .

The following day was worse still: a glacier of boredom and immobility and petty quarrelling. They had drunk the last of their vodka, and food stocks were beginning to look very scanty, given the slim hope of shooting any game *en route*. Some time during the next night one of the horses perished. When they roused themselves to the new day they found the beast lying frozen stiff under a fresh fall of snow.

However, the weather had calmed again: only a few flurries were blowing down from the grey clouds which hung low everywhere. They agreed that it would be madness to climb Khladni Ridge again and strike off northwards in an attempt to reach the centre of the explosion. Another forty versts added to the round trip could well prove suicidal.

So they loaded the two surviving horses—one of which seemed to be on its last legs, in any case—and they started the long trek southwards. Only Mirek really regretted the decision, since he still had to see his great crater; while Tsiolkovsky pointed out fastidiously, citing factors x, y and z, that there couldn't possibly be one . . .

Their return of Tolya to the bosom of the Tungusi provided a little respite on the vilest journey ever. Thereafter, it only got worse.

Before they were to struggle into Kezhma thirteen days later, they would have shot first one horse, then the second. The first, because the nag couldn't go any further—and with it, went one sledge. The second, simply for the sake of food; they had exhausted the small stock of frozen horsemeat from the first. With this second loss, they were forced to abandon the other sledge as well, along with most of their equipment, retaining only one tent, guns, notebooks and Lydia's camera. And a hunk of horse.

When they did arrive at Kezhma, the Angara River was by now a mass of swiftly moving ice-floes. But because the water hadn't yet locked solid, they bought a raft. On this they proceeded downstream, in constant danger of overturning.

Three days later they arrived at the trading station of Strelka, near where the Angara flowed out into the Yenisey; and here they rested for a while in exhaustion.

Within a week the Yenisey had frozen through thickly enough to support sleighs. So they bought two sleighs and more horses, and with a bitter wind at their backs, which presently became an Arctic blizzard, they returned to Krasnoyarsk at last down the snowy river, worn out and sick.

Ilya Sidorov was to lose his little fingers and two toes of his right foot to frostbite; while Anton was to lie ill all winter long in Countess Lydia's house, suffering from haemorrhages and vile gastric upsets due to eating half-cooked horseflesh.

However, in the Spring of 1891 Nikolai Vershinin and Lydia Zelenina would be married; and the Baron would bear her off—with her two daughters and even with the governess—to his new posting at Blagoveschensk on the River Amur just across the water from China. Here he was to command a company of Cossacks—with whom he would be transferred eight years later to Peking to garrison the foreign concession there, just in time for the Boxer Uprising, of which Lydia took some remarkable and heroic photographs during the siege . . .

And in the Spring of '91, too, after being best man at their wedding, Anton would return through the mud and floods of the Siberian plain, in the same springless rattletrap in which he had arrived in Krasnoyarsk almost a year earlier. At Perm, before boarding a steamer down the Kama to the Volga, he would manage to sell the carriage—though for a mere sixty roubles, an iniquitous loss . . .

Thirty-three

BEYOND THE WINDOWS of the Retreat, the sky was clear. Only wispy scarves of cloud still clung to the necks of the mountains. The snowy valley, with its blue blobs of dachas wearing white hats, was sharp and bright again. A snow plough sped along the twisting highway, whisking billows aside. For the fog had quite suddenly evaporated. It was Monday morning.

Victor Kirilenko and Sonya Suslova were both due back at the Psychiatric Institute in the afternoon; but meanwhile Sonya was ensconced in the small library beyond the dining room, with Mikhail. Felix presumed that the two young folk were making intimate arrangements for the future . . . Kirilenko himself was lost in thought, and Sergey was scribbling away, resentfully, at a new scenario to culminate in the awful trek back to Kezhma . . . or perhaps in the sleigh ride back to Krasnoyarsk . . . or even in Chekhov's return to Russia—though all of these options seemed sadly anti-climactic. Mikhail's concluding 'insights', into Mme Lydia Vershinina as photo-journalist of the year 1900 in Peking —at about which time the white fog had suddenly begun to lift and the outside world to re-emerge, like a photo floating in developing fluid—might well be climactic, but they were quite irrelevant to *Chekhov's Journey*, either old or new, in Felix's opinion . . . Still, something startling could be made of it all! Really, the new-style *Journey* had quite endeared itself to him—and even Sergey only grumbled mildly as he dashed off notes.

Felix was considering popping out for a brisk stroll when Mikhail appeared in the doorway, holding an open book. His hands were shaking.

"I just noticed this on the shelf . . . *Four Plays*, by Anton Chekhov. Want to hear which ones?"

Sergey raised a weary eyebrow. "That's the 1987 *People's Edition* you've got there, Mike. So what's the big deal? Think I don't know it?"

"Sergey's a bit busy at the moment." Felix fretted in case Sergey took this as an excuse to throw his pen down.

"Go on: humour me. Guess."

"*Ivanov*," said Sergey dismissively.

"Right, that's here . . . Full marks! Next one?"

"Piss off."

"No, he never wrote that. *Ivanov*'s followed by *The Apple Orchard*."

"Eh? You stupid joker!"

"Here, look for yourself! *Apple Orchard, Uncle Ivan*—and *Three Cousins*. Plus *Ivanov*, that we know and love." Mikhail headed towards Sergey, but Felix intercepted him and snatched the book away. He began turning the pages feverishly.

"But. But," he said in a lame voice.

"Now you don't suppose that I just printed the book for a giggle, in a couple of spare minutes through there? So what happened to *The Cherry Orchard*? And to *Uncle Vanya*? And *Three Sisters*? They're all gone!" Mikhail stabbed a finger towards the window. "Gone into the fog! And it's taken them off with it! It looks like a whole new world out there, returned from nowhere, eh? Believe me, it *is* a new world. These are the plays that old Anton wrote instead. Instead, damn it!"

The caretaker stood in the doorway. "Same old mountains, same dachas. So what's all the fuss about?"

"The fuss, my dear Ossy, is because Mr Chekhov now appears to have written a play entitled *The Apple Orchard*. And kindly don't tell me that apples are as good as cherries any day. Or I'll bash your brains in with the whole ruddy *Soviet Encyclopaedia*!"

For now, behind Osip, Sonya was hesitating in the hallway, scanning with a sickly look a heavy volume of that opus . . .

"The plays themselves are still pretty much the same, though!" insisted Felix, tearing the edges of pages in his haste. "Look, Ranyevskaya's still in *The Apple Orchard*. And here's Lopakhin, and Yepikhodov. Dialogue looks identical . . . Oh dear, I don't seem to recognize this bit. Anyhow, it's *much* the same—it's hard to tell, offhand."

Sergey started up, dropping pen and notebook. "See whether Vershinin, Fedotik and Rodé are still in *Three Sisters*. I mean in *Three Cousins*, damn it!"

"Half a tick . . ."

Kirilenko stared at the three men clustered round the book. "But there are much wider implications—!"

"There's no sign of them," said Felix. "Different names entirely."

"That's as you'd expect, if he based that trio on real life."

"The opening's similar. First scene. Here, this bit's exactly the same . . . Um, not here . . ."

"But these are minutiae!" Kirilenko exclaimed.

Felix looked round angrily. "The world's made up of minutiae, Victor Alexeyevich! If too many minutiae are different, just how the hell are we going to *fit in*?"

"Ah, you do realize . . . My apologies."

It was then that Sonya came forward and began to read out in a shaky voice from the biography of A. P. Chekhov in the *Soviet Encyclopaedia* . . .

So A. P. Chekhov had returned to Moscow in 1891 as something of a hero, whereas he had merely been a celebrity before he left the city. True, some radical critics still continued to carp at him, this time attacking what they described as his 'opportunism'. Nevertheless, Chekhov's report on the Tunguska Expedition—his longest published work, illustrated with photographs by L.F. Zelenina, with technical appendices by J. Mirek and K.E. Tsiolkovsky—was certainly instrumental in stimulating the haphazard exploitation of Siberian wealth in the years preceding the

Revolution, an exploitation which was only guided along socially productive lines subsequently . . .

Meanwhile, the sudden rise to prominence of the young scientist K.E. Tsiolkovsky, resulting in support for his theoretical work on cosmic flight, could be said to have paved the way for the Soviet Moon landing in 1989; while the scientist Ya. B. Morisov was stimulated by Tsiolkovsky's speculations to describe the general principles of nuclear physics, anticipating the work of Rutherford *et al* . . .

A. P. Chekhov had thus paid his dues to his 'first mistress', Science. The following years were to see his maturity as a dramatist, in *The Snow Goose*, *The Apple Orchard* and other plays. But his constitution was undermined by the rigours of the Tunguska Expedition. He soon sold the little estate at Melikhovo, to which he had moved from Moscow with his mother and sister. Poor health forced him to take up permanent residence in Yalta. And he married Olga Knipper; and he died in 1904.

His mother survived him by fourteen years; and his sister Mariya died in 1957, having served his memory faithfully for decades as curator of the Chekhov Museum which had been their home in Yalta; Mariya herself never married . . .

They digested the information in silence. By now Osip had caught on to the implications.

He scratched his head. "Obviously the Communist Party's the same. Your book mentions the Revolution. So we'll all fit in—if we keep our wits about us. We're Russians, after all."

"Imagine," said Kirilenko, "a stone thrown into a pond. The ripples die down after a little while. So Chekhov still goes to Yalta and weds Knipper and dies in 1904. By the time of the Revolution the ripples are too small to change things much. And by now, well, everything should be much the same. After all, we *did* land on the Moon last year."

"How about this nuclear physicist, Morisov?" asked Sergey.

"Doesn't the *Encyclopaedia* always go on like that? We Russians

172

invented the aeroplane before the Wright Brothers took off. We invented the helicopter. Lord knows what else."

Osip said huffily, "That's all perfectly true. Pioneer work was done."

"These plays are probably just as good as the other ones," said Felix, his mind working overtime. "I mean, he's still Chekhov, whatever else happened! And we can still make the film—about Tunguska, because it'll be absolutely *true*. Oh but hell, that means we can't use the Anton Astrov future stuff . . . It wouldn't have any point . . . *unless* we were to make a film in the '88 framework about him heading for Tunguska, and the timeship crashing—and so he finds he's *en route* for Sakhalin instead! No, wait a minute, he was *en route* for Sakhalin anyway, when he met that wretched Sidorov and heard about the explosion! It was Sidorov that started him off. But this would just be *cinema verité*—compared to our wonderful new conception!"

"I never thought it was all that wonderful," grumbled Sergey. "I just went along with the new idea to keep you happy. It was agreed we'd revert to my original scenario, if the other one crapped out. Seems to me that's all we're doing."

"Oh, but what a *loss*, dear boy!"

Kirilenko was amazed. "But surely you aren't still seriously contemplating making the film?"

"Why not? Look here, Victor: we have to cling to something to keep our sanity. We're shipwrecked—we're timewrecked. It's the only lifeboat we have, the film."

Mikhail giggled. "So take this down, Sergey old son: 'It came from outer space, into Siberia, felling a billion trees—whatever it was! Today, thanks to Anton Chekhov's investigations, Space will soon become the new Siberia, of prosperity and happiness'!" A tear appeared in Mikhail's eye. "It knocked the bloody Cherry Orchard down, it did!"

"There, there," said Felix. "We'll still make a super film, even if it *is* realistic."

"But actually . . . it was all *our* fault. *We* knocked the Cherry

Orchard down! In this building, this weekend . . . We shot the Seagull—and turned it into a Snow Goose!"

"Let's face it, Mike: wasn't Christ changed out of all recognition by those who celebrated him? Weren't his very words rewritten, even the episodes of his life? And Joan of Arc, too? And Trotsky?"

"Mr Levin!" cautioned Osip, shocked.

"Past events can be altered. History gets rewritten. Well, we've just found that this applies to the real world too." Felix tossed the copy of *Four Plays* on to the sofa and strode about. "Maybe it's happening to us all the time, without us realizing? Maybe the real history of the world is changing constantly! And why? Because history is a fiction. It's a dream in the mind of humanity, forever striving . . . towards what? Towards perfection."

"Oh yes, and how about Auschwitz?" retorted Mikhail. "And the Inquisition? And Genghis Khan? It's a grotesque parade, this world, that's all it is."

"A dream in the mind . . ." Sergey echoed Felix's words in a sinister tone. He snapped his fingers. "Might I suggest that we've all been taken for a ride—by the master hypnotist himself!"

"Sergey. Please."

"No listen, Felix. *He* hypnotised the lot of us—that's the simplest explanation! This has nothing to do with mass suggestion coming from Mikhail. Victor Kirilenko—*him*!—he hypnotised the whole bunch of us into believing that Chekhov ever did write a play called *The Cherry Orchard*. Or *Uncle Vanya*. Or *The Seagull* . . . It's that man who persuaded us the Tunguska bang happened a few years after Chekhov's death. He bloody well mesmerised us with these lies—just to see how we'd all react when the *true version* popped up out of Mikhail's subconscious, as he knew it must do. It's a psychology experiment, that's what it is—and all at our expense!"

"I suppose," said Kirilenko bitterly, "this is one way of adapting yourself psychologically . . ."

"And as for this Anton Astrov nonsense: that was because Mikhail's mind has been struggling to reconcile this farrago of lies—with what he knows deep down. I've done you an injustice, Mike!" Sergey opened his arms to embrace the actor; but Mikhail fended him off.

Kirilenko jumped up. "You do me an injustice! I really protest my innocence. Most sincerely!"

Sergey sneered. "Only animals and savages are ever sincere: so said Anton. He knew a thing or two."

"But that isn't how Dr Kirilenko proceeds," cried Sonya hotly. "Not *ever*."

Sergey ignored her. "Oh, what marvellous political applications this could have! To persuade people that things are other than they are . . . that some things never happened, and other things happened instead . . . But we'd better test it out on a small scale first, eh chaps? Something unpolitical . . . The Stanislavsky Film Unit of Krasnoyarsk seem like a good gang of dupes."

"But this is preposterous!" Kirilenko advanced, as though to break Sergey over his knee. "I demand an apology."

"And maybe, when we wake up tomorrow, we'll no longer remember *The Cherry Orchard* at all!"

Mikhail chewed at his nails; his face was haunted. "I can't star in a film, knowing all these . . . these ambiguities!" He tore a meniscus of nail loose and spat it on to the carpet.

"Yes, you must apologize, Mr Gorodsky," insisted Sonya. "What you said is grossly unfair."

"It would be a far, far better thing," said Mikhail to her softly, "if he *was* to hypnotise the whole lot of us—right now. And himself, as well! Yes, and tell us all to forget about this other Anton who wrote *The Cherry Orchard* . . . I can't bear to be haunted by mystery till the day I die."

"Is that what you really want?" shouted Kirilenko. "Oblivion? The blindfolds pulled down?"

Mikhail flapped his hands helplessly. "Look, Anton would have said that it's meaningless to blather on about a mystery. He'd have gone off, and written an . . . *Apple Orchard*, yes! An *Apple Orchard*. And he did, too . . . Speaking of which . . . I think I'll take

175

myself off somewhere quiet, and read it. Just to see what it's all about . . ." He retrieved *Four Plays* from the sofa, and slapped his jacket pocket with his free hand as though he had just slipped the book inside, though he was still clutching the volume in his other hand. "Frankly, I don't care a hang any more. It's all a grotesque parade—how can we make sense out of anything? No, you stay here, Sonya—I want to be on my own for a while."

Sonya subsided; and Mikhail departed, leaving the doors half open. Osip pulled out a pack of cigarettes. He lit one, and was promptly racked by a coughing fit.

"Oh shut up!" snapped Sergey.

"I suppose," mused Felix, "we ought to be grateful that there's *something* in the universe, rather than nothing . . . I mean, when you do come down to it: an apple orchard, instead of a cherry orchard—what's the odds? Apples or cherries? Cherries or apples? You can stew up a tasty compote with either of them . . ."

Osip thumped himself on his chest, to clear it. "Yeah, let's not get worked up in a stew. Let's keep our heads screwed on. And our feet on the ground." He flicked ash carelessly at the carpet. "Who do you reckon won the match at the Dynamo Stadium, eh?"

"Both sides lost," Sergey said sourly.

The noise of a pistol shot, coming from the direction of the library, sounded just like a champagne cork popping out of a bottle. But they all realized at once exactly what it was.

176

Thirty-four

SONYA WAS THE first through the double doors. Felix hurried after her. "It's okay! Don't panic! It's just a blank. Mike found the gun in a basket of props. He was fooling round with it earlier on. That's all it is: a prop . . ."

Sergey thrust past him. "The bloody joker, I'll settle his hash."

"It in't my fault," cried Osip, from behind. "I never knew about any pistol in them baskets, honest . . ."

But Mikhail lay sprawled out on the parquet floor of the library, amidst the gloomy mahogany bookcases and the dusty, wingback chairs draped with antimacassars. Blood was pouring from his head. His finger was still tangled in the trigger guard.

Sonya screamed, then knelt by Mikhail, rocking back and forth.

"Don't touch!" warned Felix. Urgently he turned to Osip. "Be quick, ring for an ambulance—"

"Don't do it, Osip!" shouted Sergey. "Don't be a fool! Ambulance? Police, questions? We don't know what our story is yet."

Kirilenko knelt by Mikhail, too, and felt his pulse. Then he inspected the wound closely.

"It's all right, Sonya, he's alive . . . His pulse is steady." He crouched lower. "Quiet please, everyone! He's still breathing perfectly well . . . I don't think he's in any danger. The bullet just creased his skull. It tore his scalp."

"So much *blood*—"

"Of course there's a lot of blood flow from the scalp, *Doctor*

177

Suslova! But he'll live." Kirilenko applied a handkerchief to the wound. "I'll just staunch this . . . Osip, fetch me a bowl of hot water—and I want the First Aid kit. I need scissors, dressing and plaster."

This time Osip did hurry off.

Sonya looked up. "But we *must* call an ambulance."

"Let's not react hastily. We mightn't need outside help. I'll know in a moment or so. A few minutes' delay won't harm him . . . If that gun's a stage prop, where did he get a live bullet from? Was it a lucky charm? Something he kept out of devilry?"

Stooping, Sergey eased the pistol out of Mikhail's hand. Straightening up, he broke the chamber open.

"Well, it's empty now . . . Damn it, if this was a blank pistol it oughtn't to be able to take live ammo. This isn't any prop—what's it doing here?"

"Maybe it *is* Osip's?" said Felix. "He said he didn't know anything about it—so maybe he did? Methinks the lady doth protest . . ."

"Perhaps," said Kirilenko, "it *was* a stage prop earlier on this weekend . . ."

"What do you mean by that?"

"And now it isn't. Not any longer."

"Will somebody please call an ambulance?" Sonya begged. "Or else I will."

Kirilenko gripped her arm tightly with one hand. "If you really wanted to, you'd be doing that now—not asking us. The answer's no. The bullet only grazed the bone. Maybe he'll have some concussion, and a rotten headache—but there won't be any internal damage. He's lucky."

"Is that what he is: *lucky*? So why did he *do* it?"

"Too much Chekhov on the brain," snapped Sergey. "He must have got a bloody big surprise when the gun went off."

Soon Osip bustled in with a First Aid box and a bowl of hot water. Kirilenko rummaged for scissors and began snipping away Mikhail's blood-matted hair.

While this was going on, Felix cornered the caretaker. "Do you swear you know nothing about the gun?"

"What do I want a gun for?"

"Well, how did it get here, man?"

As Kirilenko began sponging, Mikhail uttered a faint groan.

"Why, that's *Chekhov's* pistol!" Sonya exclaimed suddenly. "That's the gun he brought out to Siberia with him. Now it's been fired at last. That's it!"

"Brilliant!" Sergey fairly snarled at her. "So Chekhov left his gun behind in Krasnoyarsk—and it's been lying around in a basket ever since, waiting for us? How clever of you, Sherlock Suslova. That solves it all. *I'll* tell you what's to be done: Osip is going to take the gun out and bury it in the woods—right now. And we'll all forget about it. Okay, Ossy?"

"If the Professor says Mr Petrov's okay. . . That seems sensible. I mean, we don't want any more trouble—we've got enough on our plate as it is."

Kirilenko bandaged Mikhail's head tightly. Sergey strode over to Osip and thrust the pistol at him. Hastily Osip fumbled it away out of sight.

"We can say he slipped on the ice," said the caretaker. "Cracked his noddle, he did. That's simple enough."

Shortly, Mikhail opened his eyes and moaned. Felix bent over him. "You had a little accident, Mike."

"Uh?"

"An *accident*."

"Eh? What? Did I?"

"You did."

"Don't remember a thing—what's all this blood?"

"It's yours, dear boy. By the way, can you tell me: what *is* the last thing you remember?"

"Uh? Oh, I was thumbing through *The Apple Orchard*."

"And an apple fell down on his noddle—as on Isaac Newton's."

179

"Hush, Sergey! Now, Mike, tell me: what *is The Apple Orchard?*"

"Eh? What a thing to ask a wounded trooper." Mikhail began struggling to sit up. Kirilenko restrained him. Mikhail lay back on the parquet, squinting up. "Well, last time I was around it was a certain comedy by old Anton Pavlovich—"

"Mmm. And how about *The Cherry Orchard?*"

"Dunno. Old Antosha wrote an *Apple Orchard.* Well, he did, an' all! What are you lot staring at me for? I ain't never heard of any *Cherry Orchard.*"

"You aren't by any chance having us on, dear boy?"

"About what? Look, my head's hurting."

"My poor baby," crooned Sonya. She stroked Mikhail's cheek.

"I repeat: you aren't having us on about *The Apple Orchard?*"

"Of course I ain't having you on, you daft bugger. What am I lying on the floor for?"

"A meteor banged you on the grey matter," said Sergey. "What did you think? Happens all the time."

Sonya cradled Mikhail. "My poor baby shot himself—don't mock him."

"Shot? Myself? What with?"

"With a gun."

"Where is it, then? Show me!"

However, Osip had already ambled, crab-like, out of the library to conceal the evidence . . .

"Never mind about that," said Felix. "How about *Uncle Vanya?*"

"Eh? I haven't got any Uncle Vanya."

"Written by the well-known Mr A. P. Chekhov."

"Ah, you mean *Uncle Ivan?* Why not call a thing by its proper name? What is this, anyway: a drama quiz in a loony bin? You beat somebody over the head, and ask them stupid questions while they're lying half-witted." Reaching up, Mikhail caught hold of Kirilenko's lapel. "Is this another one of your fabulous new psycho-techniques?"

180

Firmly Kirilenko removed Mikhail's hand. "It is not. I assure you."

"And how about Commander Anton Astrov?" pursued Felix.

"Uh?"

"Of the time-ship *Tsiolkovsky*."

"I give up! You're all barmy. God, I feel dizzy." Mikhail shut his eyes tight.

"And why are we in this building, Mike—can you tell me that?"

Mikhail opened his left eye a crack. "Could it be to play charades?"

"Please be serious."

"Well, we're here to rough out the plot for a film, ain't we?"

"Yes? Carry on."

"Called *Chekhov's Journey*."

"And what's it about?"

"It's about Chekhov's bloody journey, what else? It's about his sodding Tunguska Expedition. Now, if the interrogation's quite over, can I please get up? I'll feel a lot safer up on my feet than with you lot all leering down at me."

Sonya grasped his arm, and Kirilenko took his other arm. Together they helped Mikhail up, and over to the nearest chair. His eyes watered. His bandaged head lolled against the antimacassar.

"If only you knew," murmured Sonya. "If only you knew."

"If only I knew what?"

"If I told you it wouldn't help your headache much."

Kirilenko collected up the First Aid box and his blood-stained hanky. After a moment's hesitation, he stuffed these into an empty space in one of the bookcases, directly following on the last volume of the *Collected Works* of M. M. Gorky. From somewhere outside came a faint thumping sound: Osip must be trying to hack a hole in the frozen ground with a pick or a chopping hoe, to bury the pistol . . .

"If only . . . If only I'd never come here," said Kirilenko. "But I did. So now we've collided with another world . . ."

Misunderstanding him, Mikhail rubbed his bandages ruefully. "Just as the past collided with the future, at the time of the Revolution! Or was it with my skull—eh, Sergey? Ah well: onward into the future, say I! A future of hope and happiness!" He cupped a hand behind his ear. "Hark, do I hear the jingle of the harness bells? Or is it my head that's ringing?"

"I've had horses up to *here*." Sergey made a throat-slitting gesture. "A taxi'll suit me fine . . . What am I thinking of? We've still got the Volga." He pulled out the car keys and stared at them, then bit the ignition key in the manner of a peasant testing a coin for counterfeit.

"Remember," said Felix, "the street names might have changed."

"So what? I don't doubt they'll still be the same streets. It'll be the same old world as ever—give or take the odd cherry orchard . . . Does anything ever really change?"

"My goodness," said Mikhail, "you've certainly changed your tune! You sound just like one of Anton's people. Poor burnt-out Sergey, all passion spent—and now you're exhausted. In fact," and Mikhail began to chuckle, "you sound rather like Sidorov! Possessed by an event too big for him, which nobody else even noticed till Anton came along . . . Surely a simple little film script isn't such a challenge to a professional writer?" Tears ran down Mikhail's cheeks: tears of laughter, and the strain brought a tiny, fresh spot of blood to the surface, to stain his bandage.

"Aren't you the lucky one?" cried Sergey bitterly. "*Shall* we tell him, folks?"

"Careful!" Kirilenko interposed. "Mikhail's our guide now. He's our lifeline—our interpreter, should we need one. He knows where he is. He belongs."

Mikhail carried on chortling. "You people are really too much. You're as crazy as coots!"

Like the pulse of his blood and the beat of his heart, the faint thumping continued from outside as Osip hacked away remorse-lessly at the soil, which was as hard as iron.

After a while the noise stopped. Perhaps Osip had realized that the last place to hide something was under a freshly chopped-up heap of soil, near the road.